OUT OF THE DARKNESS

a dark fairytale retelling

KC ENDERS

Copyright © 2026 by KC Enders
All rights reserved.

Visit my website at www.kcenderswrites.com
Cover Designer: Stacy Garcia, Graphics by Stacy
Edited by Hadley Finn
Proofread by Hazel James

No part of this book may be reproduced or transmitted in any form or by any means, electronic or mechanical, including photocopying, recording, or by any information storage and retrieval system without the written permission of the author, except for the use of brief quotations in a book review. No AI was used in the creation of this work, nor is permission granted in any way to use this author's work to feed or train AI.

This book is a work of fiction. Names, characters, places, and incidents either are products of the author's imagination or are used fictitiously. Any resemblance to actual persons, living or dead, events, or locales is entirely coincidental.

Print ISBN-13: 979-8-9911880-5-0

OUT OF
THE
DARKNESS

*For all the precious souls.
You're not broken, you are brave and stronger than you know.*

A Note

What would the Hundred Acre Woods be without the very ferocious, full of energy tiger and the ever anxious little piglet?

Once again, this is not a retelling, but more of a reimagining featuring some of our favorite childhood characters.

But now they're all grown up, involved with organized crime, revenge, power, and a hundred other terrible messes. For specific content warnings, please visit www.kcenderswrites.com.

...it is very hard to be brave.

Chapter 1

Pink Pompom

TRUIE

Then: seventeen years old

I click my pen closed and shove the brown leather journal back into the tree's crevice. No one is around to see, no witnesses to our hiding spot. Thank God.

Though I'm not sure how much stock I put in the big guy. I don't think his services reach this little town.

But we won't be here much longer.

This shit hole is about to be in my rearview mirror. And my best friend, Winnie, will be in the seat next to me, getting us out of here.

Days. Nothing more than a handful of days stand between us and full, beautiful, blissful freedom.

I push all the air from my lungs and start the walk back to my car. The path is shaded, the trees so thick that it feels more like nighttime as opposed to just barely dusk. Twigs snap under my feet, leaves shuffling and crunching to mark each step as I navigate down the path. On any given day, it's beautiful here. Peaceful, even. But right now, with the impending darkness, it's more than a little creepy.

I don't like it.

Something in the air shifts, and the hair on my arms stands at attention and my skin tingles.

I really don't like it.

My pace picks up, my simple walk becoming more of a slow jog. Each sound nature makes—every single sigh—takes on an ominous tone. Each innocent shadow lurking behind the trees projects some kind of nefarious intent.

Winnie told me once that she used to sleep out here when things weren't safe at home. Whether it was her parents fighting, or one of their parties, or because of strangers full of malevolence hanging around her house, the woods have always been her safe place.

It just doesn't feel that way to me.

Not now. Not as the deep, unnatural dark spreads its tendrils amongst the trees, filling every crevice with nothingness.

At the next turn in the path, the pale evening light shifts through the break in the trees, shining like a beacon. My car is right there.

Fifty yards away.

Thirty.

A relieved sigh rushes past my lips as I breach the canopy of the woods. I can't help but take a moment to appreciate the simple act of stepping into the light.

Soon, all of this worry, the uncertainty, the fear—it'll all be behind us.

Soon, Winnie and I will have the chance to start life over, to take our stash of cash from between the pages of the journal and drive away.

Soon, summers spent with my mom will become a permanent thing, and I won't ever have to see my dad again.

Thank Jesus.

I reach for the handle to pull open the door, and nothing happens. The handle lifts but the mechanism doesn't engage. It's locked. There's no reason for it to be locked. I didn't bother with it because no one ever comes out here. I'm not even sure anyone even knows this place exists other than me and Winnie.

But sure enough, when I place my hand to the window, shielding the reflection from the last rays of sun, and peer into the cup holder, my keys aren't there. They're gone.

My car is locked, and the keys are freaking gone. What kind of psycho stumbles upon a car on the edge of a trail into secluded woods and thinks *Oh, I'll do this person a favor and lock their car for them*?

And if that kind of person happens to exist in this tiny little shit town, why would they think taking the keys from that car would be a good idea?

Of all the times Winnie has needed help, not a single one of these assholes considered offering her a hand. No, she had to hope and pray that her secret guardian angel would show up when she needed them. And I can't seem to make a quick little trip in and out of this tree-infested park without my car being locked up like Fort Knox.

This is such a violation. What happened to consent? Not that it's a big priority in this town, either. We've never discussed it outright, but hints, whispers, and insinuations have been more than enough to clue me into the fact that the lack of consent is a huge factor in why my mom left. And she didn't just leave—she hauled ass to the other side of the country. Just like Winnie and

I are going to do. I'm counting down the days until that happens.

I make my way around the car, checking all four doors, looking for my keys tucked on top of or around the tires, but luck is still not my friend.

Frustrated, I round the back to check the trunk. Maybe my Good Samaritan left in unlatched with the keys inside.

I huff a laugh as I curl my fingers around the chilled metal and it gives without the least bit of resistance. My pink pompom keychain is there, but deep, deep inside.

So deep, I have to brace with my knee on the floor of the trunk and wedge myself inside to reach it. I stretch as far as I can, my fingers just grazing the pink fuzz. No matter how I wiggle, I can't seem to get enough purchase to grab them. The ring must be snagged in the carpet fibers.

A chill races down my spine as I push off the gravel and slide into the confined space, pulling at my keyring, trying to twist it free. I don't like tight spaces and wedging myself in here takes stupid amounts of self-encouragement... or I'm just stupid. I don't know, but everything about this makes me uncomfortable.

Carpet fibers and grit dig into my elbows as I shimmy further inside twisting and pulling until the metal split ring final comes free.

My sigh of relief is cut short when my foot is hoisted up, throwing me off balance. My cheek slides across the rough fabric and the sting of carpet burn blooms immediately. Tears spring to my eyes for so many reasons, not simply the raw skin marring the left side of my face. No, it's too dark in my trunk. And tight. And I didn't fall in here as a result of my own clumsiness.

"Hey!" My scream is angry, but not nearly loud enough. And the pissy *hey* should absolutely have been a loud, resounding cry for help. But I don't get the chance to try again because before I can turn over, or shimmy my way out, I feel a bee sting at the side of my neck. That's not cool because the weather is, in fact, way too chilly for bees to be out and about.

Fuck my life.

Panic washes over me as I try to push myself out of the trunk only to find I don't have the strength. I'm weak and uncoordinated.

A harsh laugh sounds from behind me as hinges creak. And I'm plunged into darkness punctuated with the unmistakable slam of the trunk closing.

My heart races, and I can't catch my breath. I'm not new to panic attacks; living with my father and his particularly cruel forms of punishment introduced me to them early on. But I've also done whatever I could to protect myself.

Because every girl living in a town like this *needs* to know the basics. Hell, we need to know the advanced stuff too.

I manage to shove the keys between my fingers, ready to swipe at whoever opens this trunk. I might be small, but I'm more than willing to fight dirty. My hand feels foreign, not just from the diminished coordination, but because there aren't enough keys. Only my first two knuckles are armored. While that's still something, and I'm sure it would suck to get hit with them, it means I'm at a disadvantage. One of the keys was deliberately removed. Then the bright happy ring was planted deep, deep, deep out of my reach.

I lash out, hitting at the door of the trunk, trying desperately to pull attention to me... *Fuck*. There's no one out here. I'm alone in the most pitifully frightening way.

It doesn't matter. I hit and kick and scream at the top of my lungs. Crying for someone to magically appear, begging to be heard, hoping to draw attention or break free from this tight prison that smells like stale tire rubber and old motor oil.

I gasp for air all while knowing I need to slow my breathing.

I fight, more with myself now, trying to find some calm so I can think rationally about how to fix this.

The engine rumbles to life, the tires almost immediately crunching against the gravel, as my car rolls forward.

With me locked firmly in the trunk.

Sweat breaks out across my skin as trembling ratchets up to full-body tremors. Though it's far too dark to see anything, I force my eyes closed, blocking out the clawing blackness and taking control of what little I can.

It takes more effort than it should to sweep my hands along the interior of the trunk, the roof of the trunk, the back of it. The plastic handle for the emergency release is gone, not even a stub of the cable remains.

Movements go from slow to clumsy, thoughts jumbling much the same. Every bump in the pitted gravel path back to the paved road tosses me around the tight space. I try to brace but weakness overtakes my control and my hands slip, arms and legs going limp, as my consciousness ebbs and flows.

God help me, I can't move. My grip on the keys fails, and they fall to the floor with a thud. I will my arm to move, or my hand, or even a finger. But paralysis sets in, and my eyes slide open, stealing the last bit of control from me.

Tears slide down my temples as the tires finally hit the paved road and the jostling stops.

I'm going to die.

Here... or somewhere else.

Fully awake.

Completely aware, but unable to do a damn thing about it.

Consumed by the darkness.

Chapter 2

Static

TEAGUE

N̲o̲t̲ ̲a̲ ̲s̲i̲n̲g̲l̲e̲ ̲f̲u̲c̲k̲i̲n̲g̲ ̲t̲h̲i̲n̲g̲ ̲h̲a̲s̲ ̲h̲a̲d̲ ̲t̲h̲e̲ ̲b̲a̲l̲l̲s̲ to go my way. Not one.

Between Christophe giving me shit while running my ass into the ground and having Truie in my bed each night but not being able to touch her the way I want, I might lose my fucking mind. Because, yeah, Truie has all but moved into my suite.

Her clothes. Her stuff. The scent of her. Her fucking essence has worked its way into my head and under my skin. She's taken over my closet, my space, my thoughts—everything. She's taken over my entire fucking life.

While I've been tied up during the day, running security and chasing after whatever shit Christophe sends my way, she's been with Winnie in one suite or the other.

It's been a stretch, but I've had to relinquish my carefully held control and put my trust in his staff to make sure she's well-tended and comfortable. And safe. That's been the hardest part of all.

As the auction loomed just on the horizon, Christophe locked his shit down while his uncle did nothing but spin further and further out of control. His special brand of instability is next level.

Christophe had me running at shit I have no idea the breadth of, knocking tasks off my list, only to find more added that made no fucking sense.

Why he thought I was the competent choice to pack up all of Winnie's shit and bring it to his office so he could supervise her while she prepared for the auction, is beyond me. The fact that he went through with it is a whole other steaming pile of shit that I don't know how to process. He knows what his uncle is, what the man does. Knows how he acquires his playthings, the vile things he does to them, and what he allows his men to do.

For the love of Christ, Alain elevated his slimy lawyer to mayor of the fucking town and then ripped his family apart. Truie's family. The only plus there was that Truie had a respite for her summers and holidays visiting her mom.

Good for her.

Shitty for me.

I spent those weeks trailing Winnie while my head was wrecked not knowing where Truie was at every goddamn moment. I had no idea how much worse it would get.

Winnie has always been my assignment, but Truie was my reward. My secret obsession born of doing a job I didn't necessarily want. Until she disappeared without a trace. Fucking killed me. And now that I have her, I don't actually *have* her. But with the auction finally done, and Christophe claiming his woman, maybe that can change.

Tomorrow, in the light of day, I'll be able to focus on Truie. Coax her to speak to me, to trust me enough to open up, or at least let me find someone who can help.

Something.

"Mr. Grey, one of the crack whores' kids is here. Wants to see Mr. Robicheaux."

I stop in the center of the foyer, my escape to my rooms and the gorgeous blonde tucked away there going up in a puff of *fuck you* that I could absolutely do without.

"Nope. Boss gave strict orders he's not to be disturbed. Whatever the kid needs, take care of it and get him out of here. We don't need anyone on the premises tonight." How did someone get on the grounds anyway? Orders were to lock down the estate after we returned from the Honey Pot.

The scrawny form of Roux Ballenger pushes through the door. "I gotta see him, Mr. Grey. It's an emergency with my ma." Distress pours off of him in waves, but that's not my problem.

Well, it is if this kid disturbs the boss.

One thing leads to another and another and a-fucking-nother and instead of sliding between the sheets and curling around Truie, I ended up cutting through the woods in tactical gear and adding a handful of names to my body count.

All in a day's work, or so they say.

I step over the threshold into Alain's home office, drawing his focus and business end of one of his men's weapons. Alain doesn't skip a beat, acting as though having the woman his nephew has killed for spread out on his lap is nothing out of the ordinary.

"Mind your tiger before he pounces and does something rash." Alain tosses his words out with a dismissive nod in my direction. "Someone could get killed with his kind of carelessness."

I've heard worse. Been called much worse by people who were supposed to mean more to me. Sometimes family isn't what it's cracked up to be, and the world is better off with them gone.

I keep still, taking in the room around me. Two of Alain's goons stand sentry. The man himself watches the hostage he has on display in front of him as he runs his mouth. Most of what I hear is just *blah blah blah*, the ramblings of a delusional old man teetering at the edge of his fall from power, but the third—maybe fourth—time he mentions the Irish, I start paying attention.

"*Le jeune homme* said he would find *le livret*. And he did not. He failed like he always does. Cocked the entire thing up and let the girl escape my stable." The way he touches Winnie, when I know deep in my soul he's talking about Truie, makes my blood boil. "So I will claim this one. She can entertain me until I get what I want back where it belongs."

Did he touch Truie like that?

Did his men?

Did my fucking cousin put a single finger on her, touch her, hurt her?

My thoughts spiral, going to a dark, dark place as I

think of all the ways I could happily make Desmond Grey suffer. Desmond and any number of his friends who I know are involved with Alain. And after taking them out, I would sleep like a fucking baby without a care in the goddamn world.

For now, though, I have to stay calm.

Doing so while surrounded by chaos is one of those random skills that's lauded in my line of work. It's never been an issue, but tonight as the overly decorated, stuffy office of the head of the French underworld descends into utter mayhem, I might be struggling.

Struggling with the shit Alain Robicheaux is tossing around against different families. Mine included.

Struggling with his admission that the asshole took out a hit his own brother to take over *le Milieu*. That he left his nephew without parents and cut him out of his due.

Struggling with the fact that if this situation goes any further south, the woman I left safely tucked in bed, the one who has consumed me, mind and soul, will be left alone, broken and without the retribution she's due. Because a single wayward twitch of an eye could have this whole thing blowing up in our faces.

And right now, it's not looking good.

"I rid this world of your father, and I will happily dispose of you in a similar fashion. All I ask for is one move, a flinch, something to assuage my complicity in your expungement." Alain's heavy French accent twists and bends around each word he utters to his nephew.

He's nothing if not a pompous motherfucker who latches on to big words in an attempt to sound smarter than he is. Though, he really did manage to hide his involvement the murder of Christophe's parents for almost a decade, so maybe he's smarter than I've given him credit for.

Christophe's tone is pained when he asks, "And *Maman?*"

"It was simple, really. And it will be even simpler to do it again and get you out of the way for—"

Two shots ring out in rapid succession from the back of the property, blowing the window and spraying glass inward. Everything slows unnaturally. On reflex, I fire my weapon and hit the sentry standing behind Alain while clocking the fact that the one who had his barrel aimed at me is in a heap on the floor, leaking profusely. Yeah, he's done.

My focus darts around the room taking note of those I care about. Christophe is up and blood free, but Winnie is still trapped in Alain's grasp, marked with splatters of crimson. A thousand little slices match the bloom of blood spreading rapidly across the white expanse of his shirt. How the shot missed her is beyond me. Glass shards glitter under the light of the heavy chandelier suspended in the center of the room. It would be beautiful if it didn't signify that something isn't right.

The majority of our men are at the front of the house, and the rest are posted around the perimeter.

"Who fired from the back?" I mumble into my comms while sprinting across the room.

The silence is broken by a sharp, "Negative, sir. Not one of ours."

My feet barely touch the balcony before I hurdle over the edge and drop to the ground, landing in a crouch that's going to fucking hurt when the adrenaline wears off.

Weapon raised, I stay low and cross the distance toward the still form in the center of the precisely manicured lawn.

"Drop it." I seethe and order on a growled command.

A gun falls to ground from a small, trembling hand. Not small, tiny. Frail and delicately made like a hummingbird's wings.

"Christ." There's only one person it can be. "Truie, love. What are you doing?" I drop to my knees in front of her and toss her gun out of reach. I'm torn between checking our surroundings and checking her for injuries.

Movement in my periphery catches my attention as

my men move in to suppress the shooter and lockdown the situation.

"Stand down. I've got this," I murmur into comms.

"But sir—"

"Fuck off out of here. I said I've got this." There's no room in my tone for misinterpretation. If anything, when we debrief, there will be a not-so-gentle reminder that orders are to be followed without question.

I shove my Glock into the waistband at my lower back and slide closer to Truie, the wet grass seeping through and soaking my knees. A chill runs through Truie as my hands hover just shy of touching her.

"Are you hurt, love? Can I touch you? Can I make sure you're okay?" I keep my voice low, soothing as I assess her, my hands skating over her palms, her arms, shoulders. They come away clean each time I look, no dark stains, no sticky blood, just a hint of moisture from the earlier rain still saturating the air.

I cup her cheek, my fingers sliding into the pale blonde curls that spring out in wild tangled ringlets, and the air shifts. For a moment, there's a hint of recognition. A small spark that I hold tenderly, much the way I hold her face between my palms and gently stoke with soft words.

"Truie, doll, you are so brave. So very brave and

you're safe now. Nothing can hurt you anymore. Not a thing, love. I've got you now…"

Her eyes lift to mine, hazy but homed in and staring deep into my soul.

"Yes, there you are. There you are. You're okay. You're safe."

I shift onto my ass and coax her to me. I guide her into my lap irrationally angry at the way her soaking wet lounge pants dare to chill her skin and make her uncomfortable. My intentions might be good, but something in my actions, or my pinched features, cracks the tenuous hold she has on herself. And as quickly as she locked in on me, she's gone.

"Truie, come back to me. Don't drift away *a cuisle*. Look at me, come on. I need you here with me," I plead, desperate to have that light back. But I've lost her again to the darkness inside her.

My shoulders sag under the weight of— What is this? Failure? Yeah, feels like failure, like I missed something, didn't grab the spark of her quickly enough, hold tight enough. Keep her from drifting away. But how am I supposed to do that when she's so goddamn fragile that the slightest step in the wrong direction pushes her away.

She needs calm and steady, and I'm a staticky ball of barely contained chaos under pressure.

With her body held securely to mine, I stand and march Truie through the dense woods that separate Alain's estate from Christophe's. It's not efficient, it sure as fuck isn't fast, but it's an opportunity to burn away some of that static. It's also a guaranteed way to keep her close, to ensure I don't have to let her go. An irrefutable reason to keep her for myself, even if just for a short time. Because seeing the light in her eyes fade into fear and then nothingness solidifies that I'm not what she needs.

Chapter 3

Taken

TRUIE

My head is fuzzy, and my body hurts. I'm exhausted like every muscle has been coiled tight, strained, and trembling for far too long.

Or like I've been running for my life.

I don't run. Been there, tried that once upon a time.

It didn't work out all that great for me back then and I doubt anything's changed.

Instead, gentle rocking pulls me back from the edge of darkness, the corners in my mind where I go to escape when things get hard and scary. Someone normal might be lulled to sleep with this kind of thing, but for me the repetitive motion soothes. Why? Because I'm a fucking conundrum.

Strong but fragile.

Here but disassociated.

Broken but breathing.

Alive but terrified to live.

So I hide in the darkness, in my dreams, and in the silence that always seems to accompany them. It's safer there. Or at least it seems that way. Safety is a concept I lost my grasp on long ago. It was ripped away from me along with what was left of my innocence and almost all of my trust.

It may not be the smartest move, but experience has taught me to be still. To use whatever senses I have access to and take in as much information as I can.

God, the lessons I've learned on being kidnapped, drugged, beaten, and... Yeah, it's the *and* that fucks me up every time. The other shit? I could fill a book with that or talk for hours on the subject and still not come close to sharing all of those experiences.

But here? Right now? This? This is comfortable. This feels okay. *This* feels like strong arms cradling me and holding me close. Secure without being suffocating. Not restrictive. Not holding me down and preventing me from moving.

It feels like a dream. Like *my* dream.

"Are you back then?"

The question rumbles through my body as much as

I hear it. And the voice is the one that's soothed me over the past few days. It has only been days, right? Days since the thin thread holding me here in this town snapped. Days since I rocked on the landing of the stairs in Winnie's house, waiting for her parents to come down off their high. Days since my best friend sent me into the woods while she called the police when it became obvious the syringes hanging from their lifeless arms signified hope. Days since we stood side by side in the cemetery, biding time and playing our parts until we could run and finally leave this town behind us.

That was the plan. To leave and never come back. To put everything that happened behind us and start over. Reinvent ourselves and... And what? Winnie has her shit together, she could do all of those things.

Me? I'm not so fortunate or free. I have a ton of baggage holding me back. My terror. My anxiety. My absolute fucking fear of anything and everything.

"It's okay if you're not ready to talk, but you should know that you're safe. It's over now. I've got you." The rumble of that deep voice soothes. The cadence, the slightly lyrical lilt...

Winnie is the only person I've been comfortable enough with to speak for a long time. The stuttering I managed to conquer as a child, reared its ugly head and dug its filthy talons in tight since I've been back. Who am I kidding? It's been since I was taken.

Taken. While that word is perfectly adequate to describe what happened to me, it's not enough. Not big enough, expansive enough… just, not enough.

It became infinitely easier to just stay silent. Keep quiet. Make myself small and disappear, but on my terms.

This, though? My terms were not taken into consideration for whatever this is. God, what is this?

A shift and a moment of weightlessness, has me jostled higher in the arms that cradle me so carefully against a solid wall of muscle. A wall of muscle that smells like sunshine and sin. It smells like rain and freshly cut grass, like the promise of summer.

And security.

Somehow, over the past days—or week, maybe—this scent has become the one I associate with being safe and cared for. Jesus, how long has it been since I've felt those things or anything remotely close to it?

Too long. Way too freaking long.

I sink down, immersing myself in it. Letting the calm flow over me like a balm, wrap me up, and keep the chaos at bay. I allow myself to think, to sift through what I know, so I can prepare for what comes next. Because God knows, I will never let my guard down again. I can't. Been there, done that. And it's a hard no thank you to the participation t-shirt for any of those past adventures.

Or this current one, if I'm totally honest.

Bits and pieces of the world outside my head manage to slip through the barriers in my mind. We didn't go back home after burying Winnie's parents, but once panic set in at the cemetery, a lot of what went down is just not there. It's vanished. We sure as hell didn't get into her car and drive away. That plan got fucked hard for the second time in our lives.

I hate that I lose time. I hate that even simple things tend to float away or get twisted into ruined snippets of memories that don't fit together. I hate how what's happened to me has the power to rule me.

I crack open an eye to see if anything can shake something loose in my brain, but all I see are the dark looming silhouettes of trees. The woods are too thick, too dark for us to be anywhere else but still here. Always here.

Winnie was on alert, almost panicked as we watched that figure stalk toward us in the cemetery. I felt a shift in my bones then, and as much as I trust it was for good reason, Winnie getting spun up sent me deeper into my abyss. It does that now.

I used to be the strong one, the stable one. The one

who stood sentry and made sure nothing bad came down on my best friend. Now I barely qualify as functional.

But that... that should be changing, shouldn't it? The weight that's become my constant companion should be lifting now because...

"I-i-is he d-d-dead?" I ask. My voice, barely above a whisper, is rough and uncomfortable. I want to pull the question back, to swallow down my words and crumble in on myself. Less for the confirmation I seek, more for the fact that it might not be true. Because while conquering that monster is a step in the right direction, this shit is far from over. Really, really far.

The man carrying me pauses, his steady steps stuttering for just a moment before continuing forward, strong and sure. The arm around my back tightens briefly before relaxing again, almost like he knows that holding me too tightly is a bad thing.

"Alain? Yeah, he's gone."

I tense. Every muscle goes taut, my breath stutters, catching in my chest. My vision goes dark at the edges, and fear presses in all around me.

"G-g-gone? Not d-d-d-d—"

I can't. I can't do this. Can't keep living under the heavy crush of fear that's ruled my life since I was taken. I'd been so certain my shot had hit him. So fucking certain and now...

"Dead. He's dead, love." His soft gaze rakes over me before he picks up his pace, moving briskly through this void. "Are you okay hearing that? Does it disturb you?"

Reality crashes over me. I spoke to this guy. I looked at him directly enough to note that *he* looked at *me*. Is this my brain twisting shit up on me? Is this real? God, I have no idea. My cheek warms as I shake my head, his black shirt soft against my skin.

He's blissfully silent as he continues stalking through the dense woods, giving me space I desperately need to try to make sense of things. I should be scared. I know this beyond the shadow of a doubt because I'm still here. I'm still in this town, in the arms of a man I recognize but don't remember. Held captive, both literally and figuratively.

But I'm not.

Deep down, in the recesses of my cold, broken, black heart, there's a spark of something warm and familiar. Something that hints at the end. The question is: Which one?

Chapter 4
Technicality

TEAGUE

We walk through the dense woods from Alain's expansive estate toward his nephew's mansion. How Christophe has lived so close to that monster for so long, I have no idea. If I weren't inextricably tied to the man, I'd have bounced a long time ago.

But I am.

So, I'm still here. Sifting through the family businesses and sorting out details that no one fucking wants to dive into. And I have a front row seat to the shit and depravity that brought a bright smile to a horrible man's face. Watching that light dim into fear made my fucking day.

Did I lie when I told her he was dead? Maybe, but it

was honestly a technicality. There's no way he'll be anything but cold, gray, and lifeless by the time Christophe leaves that estate tonight.

The weight of that deception is heavy. This woman in my arms, not so much.

Though hearing her voice—that sad, timid sound so heavily laced with unimaginable fear and anxiety—damn near brought me to my knees. But she has that power over me. She has for a very long time.

The back of the mansion is lit up like it's Christmas, or like a jail break is in full swing and the perimeter lights are the only hope of finding the escapees.

I don't like it. It's going to draw too much attention. Bring the wrong people to us. People looking for information and willing to do whatever it takes to get it. And they've already amassed a laundry list of vile things they don't lose any sleep over to get what they're after.

Nothing like being up against the zero-conscience brigade.

I've done some sketchy shit in my life—had to in order to do my job—but even I have limits.

Or I did.

But now? For Truie? Those limits may as well be fractured fairy tales.

I pause in the shadows, the expansive lawn in front

of me, lights glaring. This isn't good. The minute I step out of the darkness, I'm a sitting duck.

A tremble, more like a shiver, slides through Truie, and she burrows further into me. I didn't think she could get any closer, but she manages. Almost like she trying to crawl inside me.

"Cold or scared?" I ask, voice low and eyes scanning. My weapon is within easy reach, but if I need it, I have to let go of the woman in my arms, and I don't know that I can. Even if it's to protect her.

"B-b-both?" She's killing me, this one. But hearing her voice, finally after so, so long, is like a birdsong. I mean, I've heard it, but always in quiet conversation with Winnie when I was out of her line of sight. Never when she could see me. Never directly to me.

"I need you to wrap your arms around my neck. Can you do that for me?" I get a nod this time, but nothing else. That's good enough for now. "Hold tight. I have to grab something quickly, and then we'll get moving again. Get you in the house, warm and safe, yeah?"

Delicate arms unfurl from where they've been tightly tucked against my chest, trapped between our bodies. One spools over my shoulder and wraps around my neck, a cool dry palm against my heated skin.

With more strength than I could've ever imagined her possessing, Truie pulls herself higher on my chest, twining her other arm around me, and holds on for dear life. Like I'm the only thing between her and the monsters who have been nipping at her heels.

"You solid? Don't let go unless I tell you."

Her face is tucked into the crook of my neck, arms holding her securely to me. If it weren't for the trail of bodies already being cleaned up behind us, and the fact that I'm reaching for my gun, this moment could almost be sweet. Romantic. I like the feel of her wrapped around me.

I shift, trying to take some of the burden of support from her, and pull the Glock from the small of my back.

I speak into my comms, "Kill the lights. I'm coming in."

"Sir?"

"From the back. I'm coming across the lawn and have Miss Cochonette with me. I need the lights taken down and the back entrance ready to breach." I want to rip out someone's throat for the simple fact that she was able to slip out of the house undetected. I want to lay the guy who was supposed to protect her low and offer him the opportunity to feel the same swirl of panicked fear-riddled anxiety I imagine Truie felt leaving the house, stealing across the lawn, finding her way through the woods, all to what? Kill Alain? Was that her goal? How did she know what we were doing or where we were going? How did she get a fucking gun? I have so many questions.

The okay comes quickly as the lights blink out, shrouding us in darkness and providing cover for our trek across the exposed expanse.

My eyes never stop moving. Every shift of light, every sway of the trees surrounding us, every single thing is noted, assessed, and filed away.

The relief that crashes over me as I push through the back entrance and into the hallway is almost a shock to my system. I'm not ready for it. I don't want it yet. I need the buzz to maintain my focus.

The door clicks softly behind us, and we're met with nothing but silence. At least at this end of the house. I'm sure the opposite wing is pure barely contained chaos. Debriefs, assessments, war council, because that's what this fucking is, or what it was, what it has been for a long time coming.

A fucking war of Alain Robicheaux's creation.

Whatever relief or calm I feel goes up in flames as Truie tenses in my arms. The calm and quiet spin her up, and stress her out.

"You're good, remember? I've got you." It's nonsense said to make her feel better, sure, but is that all it is? No, not even close. "We'll get you tucked away in my suite and get you warm." This was my fucking mistake.

When all hell broke loose, Truie was in her suite, not mine. I made the piss-poor assumption that she would be okay there, that the mansion was enforced strongly enough to keep the monsters at bay. It never crossed my mind that she would cut and run. That wouldn't have happened if she'd been in my suite. It shouldn't have fucking happened at all.

This one fucking night one woman was stolen... and another stole away. That shit won't stand.

The mechanisms whir when I press my hand to the panel on the wall and the lock clicks granting me access to my suite. Inside, I close the door and make a full sweep of the space. If the last several hours have shown me nothing else, it's that there is no such thing as too careful. Satisfied that my rooms are secure, I set my Glock on the side table and wrap my arm around Truie again.

It feels good. Having her in my arms, knowing that she's right here, and I don't need to worry about her falling or letting go. She's safe here and that... That's...

Jesus, she's got me tongue tied in my own damn head.

I stride through the sitting room and bedroom, only stopping once we're in the en suite.

She's shivering. Her whole body is shaking and trembling, and while I know that's kind of her thing, the mud on her clothes and the outside temperature sure as shit aren't helping the situation.

I pause in the center of the room, not sure which option is best. Or how I need to go about this, really. "Shower or bath?"

Truie tenses briefly before shifting her head from its place tucked against my neck. Her eyes meet mine in the black framed mirror above the vanity. There's a lot there but oddly enough, not blatant terror. It's been a rough week for this girl, so I'm taking that as a win.

Time drags out with no answer, and as much as I would love to stand here all night, to do whatever it takes to put this little bird at ease, I have work shit to deal with.

"To warm up, love. Do you want to soak in the bath or get in the steam shower?"

"I-I-I d-d-d-on't—" Her lips press together in a thin hard line as her words stick in her throat.

"I don't want to push you and I don't want you uncomfortable—I'll step out as soon as we have you set, but we need to get you clean and warm before I go take care of some things," I explain.

Her gaze snaps to mine, and it's filled with mild panic. Blown pupils. A little bit glassy. This is what I want to avoid with her. This girl has been through shit that no one should ever have to think about... let alone endure. I don't know the details, but I saw where she was being held. I hold no illusions about how terrifying it was.

"Do you want me to have one of the maids come help you?"

The dissent is nothing more than a tight shake of her head. "W-winnie?"

"No, love. She's not able to be with you right now. But we'll arrange to see her as soon as we can, okay?"

She rolls her lips between her teeth and shifts her gaze away.

"Okay." My deep breath has her rising with my expanding chest. "Bath?" I prod.

I don't have time to sit here while she takes a leisurely soak. Every minute I stand here means more and more shit piling up on my to-do list.

Another tight shake has me nodding. And thank God for that.

"Shower, then?" As the question falls, I'm already moving around the en suite gathering anything she might need—a towel, wash cloth, the fluffy robe that I don't think I've ever used. Not sure how it even got here. I set them all on the small bench just outside the shower door.

I reach into the glass enclosure to flip the taps and adjust the temperature, hoping it's in the neighborhood of what she wants. And then, after a gentle squeeze, I set Truie on her feet.

She hesitates before releasing her hold on me and immediately folds in on herself. Shoulders high and forward, arms crossed protectively around her torso, gaze locked on her feet.

I hate it. Hate everything about the way she crumbles inward.

The battle I fight in my head is epic—to stay or go, to scoop her back up and say fuck it to everything else. I have to tear myself away, step out of the room, and give her some privacy. God knows I have no business being in here while she showers. So I'm not sure who I'm actually trying to reassure when I say, "I'm going to step out—just into the bedroom and get you something to wear, yeah? You get cleaned up and warm, and I'll be right out there when you're done."

The eyes on this woman. They fucking slay me. Big, wide, full of innocence and fear, terror and pleading. They're enough to bring me to my knees. Slay a dragon. No, fuck slaying the dragon, I want to kill her monsters and lay their severed heads at her feet in a nice neat little line.

Another big breath has my chest expanding, and I blow out all of that air from my body. Unremarkably, it does nothing for my stress.

"Okay, you're good?"

The lack of back and forth is hard, but I get it, not being able to get her words to cooperate has to be a real mindfuck for her. Stress on top of stress. Good times.

I step out of the bathroom and pull the door closed behind me.

What am I doing? How did I get here, juggling a tiny, fragile woman, a newly minted crime boss, and metric shit ton of complications?

My palm just clears my eyes as I pull my hand down my face when I see Truie. She's standing in the bathroom, door barely cracked, as she peers through the small opening.

"Still here," I say. "Latch the door, love. Lock it if that makes you feel better, but I'll be right here until you're done, just like I promised."

Her gaze stays fixed on mine as the gap slowly closes. The click of the mechanism sliding into place is an auditory exclamation point.

That barrier is strictly for her peace of mind, to give her the illusion of safety, security, and control. Because if something happens, if this house catches fire or there is some other fucking emergency tonight, there isn't a lock in the world that could keep me from getting to her.

Chapter 5

Blood

TRUIE

I stand in the center of Teague's bathroom, arms wrapped tightly around myself, fighting not to come undone.

It's hard. Really hard.

But I'm here.

And Alain is dead.

That's one.

It takes everything I have to fight the urge to check the lock on the door for the third time. I'd happily go for a fourth. If there were a chair in here, a little stool—anything heftier than a stack of towels—I'd shove that up against the door too.

Yes. I'm broken.

I am completely and totally fucked up.

Can't string words together anymore to save my life.

But I'll kill myself trying to survive. *Isn't that a twist worth pondering?*

Sadly, there's nothing to fortify the door, so I have to have faith. That's something I'm wildly unfamiliar with.

Steam swirls in the shower, spilling out into the massive bathroom and drawing me into its warmth.

When Teague offered the option of soaking in a hot bath, a part of my soul thawed. I would love to sit in hot, fragrant water. Let the scents and heat seep into my bones and melt away the tension that has become a permanent fixture in my muscles... and in my life. But I can't.

It's not... I don't know... safe?

Prudent is more like it. A good idea might be even more accurate. But the real kick of it is, I would be way too exposed. Vulnerable.

So I strip off my tattered, dirty clothes and practically launch myself into the shower. I brace, expecting the water to scald but the billowing clouds of steam are just that, but the water itself is the perfect temperature—not too warm and certainly not a hint of cold.

The parallel to Goldilocks and her bears does not escape me. A giggle threatens to bubble up at the absolute ridiculousness. If I were a different person, I would let it and revel in the silly comparison. But I'm not. Goldilocks had opportunity on her side, choices when it came to tasting her porridge, and got to pick the bed she ended up in. I haven't been nearly that lucky.

Instead of lingering, I wash quickly, never taking my focus off the door. I locked it, yes, but I'm not naïve enough to think that a simple piece of metal will keep the monsters away. Locking it was symbolic. A test. And the fact the door remains closed surprises me. *Pfft.* Shocks me, is more like it.

I dry off and slip my arms into the bathrobe, wrapping it around me as tightly as I can. The thing is huge. Obviously, because the man who lives in these rooms is as well. But the material is thick and soft and warmer than it has any right to be. But it's not practical, not when I need to be ready. Not when I might have to run.

Slowly, and oh so carefully, I open the door and peek out into the room.

"Feel better?" Teague asks from the other side of the bed.

My gaze darts around, taking in as many details as I can manage.

He checks his watch, glances at the small pile of clothes neatly folded on the edge of the bed, and tilts his head like he's listening to something only he can hear.

And he's across the room. Not crowding my space. Not looming. Not threatening in any way at all.

My body buzzes, flight and fight at war with the fall back to freeze.

"Those might be more comfortable." He nods toward the bed. "It's just a t-shirt and some lounge pants. That robe looks like it's about to swallow you whole."

I nod because words are stupid when they're stuck and won't cooperate. The urge to fidget is strong, but I stuff it down. Only prey understands just how important stillness is when a predator is watching. And after all I've been through, it's wise to assume everyone is a predator.

The moment drags out as he watches me. And me? I keep my eyes peeled for any indication he's going to pounce.

"I'll, uh…" His whole body seems to expand with his breath before he blows it out again. "I'll step out so you can change." He turns and walks out of the room, swinging the door behind him.

Everything this guy does has me tilting on my axis. Like I'm caged but consulted on what kind of bars I want. Restrained, but respected? That can't be right. It can't be. All of this is just smoke and mirrors, lulling me into that false sense of security before the bottom drops out and I have to retreat into myself again just to survive.

My survival strategy does not include getting voluntarily naked unless I'm behind locked doors. I haven't been able to do that for years. And this door isn't merely unlocked; it didn't even close all the way behind him.

Shit. Shit. Shit.

But this robe is cumbersome. It's a problem for me and as much as I would love to hide, I need to be able to move freely. I hold up the lounge pants and stare at them, thinking this room is familiar, like I've spent time here. Or maybe that's just my brain playing with trauma trying to trip me up again.

On silent feet, I tiptoe to the dresser and slide open the top left drawer. Familiar leggings are rolled neatly in a line of pretty shades of pink. I pluck a pair out and slide them on instead. For my top, though, I'm sticking with the oversized option Teague left in the pile for me.

I glance at the door and give myself a pep talk worthy of something much greater than pulling on a t-shirt, but here we are and this needs to happen. So, I drop the robe and pull the soft gray fabric over my head. The shirt is so big, I get kind of lost in it. The fabric tightens as I twist it around looking for a way out. I shove my arm through a hole, fairly certain it's a sleeve, when I hear voices.

I twist and shimmy as the internal buzz increases.

This is why I need the doors closed, locked. Secure... -*ish*.

I can't see.

I'm stuck in gray cotton, and the twisted shirt is becoming more and more like a full body restraint—a straitjacket. Air saws in and out of my lungs, faster and faster, becoming way too shallow to supply enough oxygen. Passing out is not an option today. Not now.

The voices from the other room dip low, but anger laces through them both.

I finally manage to shove my head through the neck and pull the shirt into place when Teague lets out a sharp, "Fuck. Son of a bitch. Go. I'm right behind you."

I peer through the gap and everything about him screams anger. His tight shoulders, the clenched fists at his sides, and the red flush on the apples of his cheeks.

I bet he hates that tell.

I step back into the shadows when he looks in my direction, hoping that the movement isn't enough to draw his attention. But he stalks out the door behind the older gentleman I've seen working in my time here. His name is there, just out of my reach. I know him, but I don't.

The door swings slowly on its hinges, stopping with the latch resting against the doorjamb.

It's open.

The door is open.

It's open, and no one is reaching back to close it.

Silently, once again, I tiptoe through the sitting room and pause with my shoulder pressed against the wall. Listening. Waiting.

And no one is coming to close it.

I pull on the handle and peer out into the hall. Muffled voices drift down from the right, growing quieter as they flit away. Staying close to the wall, I trail after the voices. I've walked these halls more than once, though always with an escort, but I memorized what I was able. When I pass Winnie's room, things become unfamiliar.

Unfamiliar is scary.

Unfamiliar is terrifying.

But the voices pull at me, drawing me closer instead of driving me in on myself.

This is insane—I should be snooping, learning more of the layout of the house and looking for a way out while everyone is occupied. What is wrong with me?

Ahead, the hall opens into a grand entryway with ornate rugs, dark wood, soft lighting, and it's full of people. I press myself into the corner just out of sight and wait. One breath, then another, but no one's looking in my direction.

No one pays any attention to me, if they even know I'm here.

"We got a body leaking in the house next door and you're telling me you don't know anything? Didn't hear anything?" The gruff voice is familiar. Ice crawls up my spine and wraps its ugly hands around my throat, choking me.

"Don't know what to tell you, Des. We're far enough away out here, we don't hear much." Teague's voice changes, taking on a lighter tone, but the levity is forced. Strained. "Try to be good neighbors… Mind our own business. Know what I mean?"

"Good neighbors don't hear gunshots? Don't report that to the authorities?"

"Gunshots? Is that what that noise was?" The other man scoffs, but Teague continues, "And tone it down, you're a fucking beat cop, bought, paid for, and owned."

"You know what a gunshot sounds like, Tig. Don't bullshit me. Lying to an officer of the law isn't a wise choice."

The implied threat is unmistakable.

"Officer of the law," Teague mumbles low. "I remember when you were still shitting your pants at every damn holiday, so don't with me."

Teague knows him.

The icy band around my neck tightens, and blood whooshes through my ears.

I know him.

I push myself further into the corner, making myself as small as I possibly can.

That voice.

I want to run, put as much space between me and its owner as I can, but my legs won't move. They can't.

That... that man.

My back slides down the wall, slowly—torturously slow—until my backside hits the floor.

I suck in a deep breath and chance a look at him.

His face. The way his eyes would light up and darken ominously, all at the same time.

I curl into myself and tuck my face against my bent knees.

The way he'd grin when he pressed his knife against my skin.

His excitement when the first slice would well up with bright red dots that multiplied into a fine line before overflowing.

The way he'd run his finger through my blood, painting it along my thighs, my stomach, my breasts.

The thrill he got watching my fear take control.

The way he held his breath, the anticipation that vibrated off him until my first tear fell.

The whispered *yes* as others followed, pooling in my ears, wetting my hair.

The sharp sound of metal teeth separating as he lowered his zipper.

The way he'd paint his erection with my blood. With my pain.

And he's *here*.

He's standing in the foyer of the house I've been staying in, talking to the man who's brought me the only sense of security I've felt in years. Asking about the man I most definitely killed tonight.

My hearing becomes fuzzy and muffled. My vision goes hazy and dark. And all I know—all I can register—is fear and panic.

I don't know how long I sit curled in a tight ball, but it feels like a lifetime and no longer than the blink of an eye. I'm too scared to move, too rigid to rock, too panicked to breathe. I just close my eyes and pray to the God who hasn't listened to me for years, that this all just goes away. My wild act of brash foolishness is about to sink its teeth into my narrow ass.

"Jesus Christ, how did we fucking lose her twice in one night?" The normally soft, soothing voice I've come to yearn for is sharp and full of anger.

I sink in further on myself all while finally becoming aware of my surroundings again. Every muscle is coiled tight, painful in its rigidity, as I curl in with all my might. If I could just disappear, none of this would matter. If I could fade away, I wouldn't have to feel the pain or this fear ever again.

I squeeze my eyes shut and count the seconds as they tick by.

"How did she get out of the suite?"

"I don't know, Mr. Grey. Are we certain the door closed fully behind you?"

"Obviously not. Jesus fucking Chr—"

"Have you checked the CCTV? Perhaps..."

The voices are louder now, closer. But there's nowhere for me to go. Not that I could even force myself to move.

I have nothing left.

I have no one.

I've lost everything, everyone.

"Sir?" This voice is soft, accented, and it sounds like the owner is standing very, very close. Maybe even close enough that I could touch them if I were to reach out. "It looks as though we've a little lost bird here."

The air around me shifts, the stark edges of fear softening, rounding into something decidedly less awful.

Relief smooths the frenetic tone as a familiar presence drops down next to me. "Little hummingbird, how did you get free?"

Chapter 6

Silhouettes

TEAGUE

Desmond Grey fucks up everything he touches. Every single thing. And seeing Truie curled in on herself, tighter than she was after killing a man, speaks volumes.

When I gather her in my arms, there's no give. No melting into my hold.

"Shall I prepare a bath for Miss Cochonette, sir? Perhaps," Garrick pauses, probably thinking hard about what he's about to say. "Perhaps a call to Hibou is in order?"

God, I wish I knew. Calling in our doctor is the easy answer. A sedative-filled needle would have Truie pliant and relaxed in no time, but it's become a thing of convenience. A crutch. I know it works, but her drug-induced compliance is the last thing I want.

Maybe the last thing she needs.

"No to the bath, we just did that after getting back from—" I cut myself off, realizing I've already said much more than I needed to. "And not just yet on Hibou."

I debate my next move, although there's really no question which way this needs to go. My suite and hers are familiar, probably more likely to offer enough security for Truie to let go a little if I actually close the fucking door behind me. But there are things I have to do in Christophe's stead. There's no way in hell I'm disturbing him now. Not a chance.

Instead, I turn toward Christophe's office taking Truie with me. "Are the decanters filled? The humidor? If I have to call Eddie to come in this late..."

"Of course, sir. And I'll prepare a light plate or two," Garrick finishes my thought as if it's common practice to call in our legal counsel in the small hours of the morning.

Some days it is, but not often. And when it does happen, shit's bad.

Maneuvering behind the massive desk is a challenge with my hands occupied with precious cargo. When I have us as settled as possible in the boss's chair, I reach for my phone and send the summons, burying my nose in the cloud of pale curls, breathing Truie in as I wait.

I don't have to wait long. Mere moments after Garrick deposits a tray on the edge of the desk, Edmond Émile Yore III, drops into the chair across from me.

"What the actual fuck this time?" is how he chooses to greet me.

Is it brusque? Yes.

Is that well-earned? That would also be a solid yes.

Eddie accepts the offered whiskey and downs it in one go, then holds the glass out for Garrick to refill. This is how we do late night business, though there's never been a woman my lap before.

I make a concerted effort to keep my body relaxed. "We've got a problem."

"No shit," he says peering at the tray full of food that was presented to him at this stupid time of night... or morning. "Looks like you have more than just the one."

My sharp exhale disturbs the white-gold curls that obscure Truie's face from view. "Wouldn't drag you out of bed this late for anything less than a shitstorm."

"That's bullshit and you know it. Where's the bossman? Getting his beauty sleep or sleeping with a beauty?"

I shift the chair so Truie's facing away from him. Protecting her is paramount, not that Eddie's a threat.

"Not to be disturbed under any circumstances." He'll know soon enough that Christophe's priorities have shifted as much as the family's leadership has. "Alain's dead, and a good number of his men too."

He huffs a laugh and pops a brow, because to him, this isn't really that big of a deal. "So you need Lapin to clean that shit up. This"—he circles his finger in the air between us—"can wait for business hours." He stands to take his leave.

"Sit," I bite out, surprised when he tilts his head and considers whether he will or will not. "Desmond showed up way too fast and far happier than he has any right to be when the man who signs his paycheck was rapidly reaching room temperature."

I don't miss the way his gaze drops to Truie, to the way my arms band protectively around her. "She have something to do with it?"

I don't confirm or deny, just give him a small dip of my chin. This is all part of the dance we do exchanging information. Just a little but not too much. Never more than he needs to know.

Eddie snags a tart from the platter and pops it into his mouth, chewing far longer than the bite-sized treat requires while he no doubt ponders his next question. "Much as I hate it, I think I need to know what went down. Is this issue tied to the invitation-only event at

The Honey Pot, or is it something"—his head tilts side to side, gaze drifting back to Truie—"more?"

"Yes."

He shoves his hand through his hair, pulling the long strands back from his face. "Spill."

Now it's my turn to choose careful words. Because while Eddie's asking for more information, he doesn't want the full story. Nothing he doesn't *have* to know. And I don't know how much of this conversation Truie is taking in. The last thing I want is to send her deeper into her darkness.

"He seemed less concerned with the dead bodies than he should be, though I don't doubt for a heartbeat that he'll use them to get what he wants."

"And what is it that he wants? Or do I not want to know?"

"He's looking for a file. Alain mentioned something about a book," I offer. My voice is purposely low, but the body pressed against me tenses almost indiscernibly, her shallow breaths stuttering before resuming.

"A book." It's not a question, so Eddie must know. "*The* book," he adds.

"Yeah?" As much as I want to hit this with the kind of deep dive I usually reserve for special jobs, I hold back, because protecting Truie means more to me right now.

Impatience and frustration drip from the man. "And?"

I shake my head.

He nods toward Truie, the silent question perfectly clear, though I'm not sure how clear my shrug and head tilt are as a response. Not until he sinks lower in his chair and folds in on himself in defeat.

"Fucking hell." Eddie raises his glass and drinks deeply. "So Alain is dead, the file is still missing, and Christophe finally has his honeybee. Want to tell me about what's happening here?" He lifts his chin at me, sitting behind the boss's desk with a beyond scared, utterly silent, trembling woman on my lap.

I let the question hang between us while Eddie taps angrily at the screen of his phone. Only when he sets it face down on his thigh and gives me his full attention do I respond.

"Remember the girl who was taken several years ago, the one who showed up out of nowhere and didn't speak? She was living with the L'Oursons until they OD'd. Well, she was at the cemetery with Winnie when Christophe went to collect his debt, and here we are."

"She been here the entire time?" He asks a vague enough question, I give him a *yep* and nothing more. Technically the two estates are attached, so here and there are really all the same, and there is no way I'm giving her up. No way I'm not going to stand up and protect her with all I have. "And you have nothing more for me?"

"Not now. Though we should verify that the security footage at both locations has been wiped." Our guys know the protocol, but we need to control this situation and the narrative surrounding it. Make sure nothing gets leaked that we don't want out there.

Eddie scowls at his phone and heaves out a sigh that carries the weight of the world with it. There's only one thing that pulls that weariness over him like a little black rain cloud—his ex.

"Amie stirring up shit over Evie?" There should be an *again* tacked onto the end of that question, but that's not a scab I want to pick at right now. Not when I have my own pile to deal with.

"Every chance she gets." He pushes to his feet and rounds the chair he just vacated. "When are you free to go over the details? We need to get fully synced before shit blows up in our faces."

"Give me a couple hours. Let me get her settled and get Christophe up to speed. Crash here, if that's easier for you," I offer, fully expecting him to do just that.

But Eddie pulls his phone from his pocket and frowns at it again before turning and stalking from the room. "Text me a time when you've got one. Sooner is better." And then he's gone, leaving me with more questions.

Silence settles in as the sky begins to lighten, the silhouettes of individual trees stepping out of the darkness. And the rigid ball of tension in my lap softens.

Bit by bit, minute by minute, she uncoils. Every pass my hand makes from her ankle to knee and back again has her muscles thawing. She's got to be exhausted. That level of sympathetic response is a lot, the full-on freeze, non-responsive, kick-you-in-the-ass kind of a lot.

It seems like, in the blink of an eye, the progress we've made since bringing the girls here has come completely undone, but instead of a neat tidy spool to deal with, it's become a tangled mess. And I can't put my finger on the point around which we pivoted.

As gently as I can manage, I lean us forward so I can reach the tray Eddie barely touched. I slide it closer, within easy reach when I sink back into my chair, because this girl needs to eat. She's so slight. Holding herself that tight has got to use some serious energy, and she does not have anything extra on her to burn.

I stack some cheese and prosciutto on a cracker and offer it to her. It feels like an absolute dick move, trying to feed a grown-ass adult what amounts to a childhood snacky-snack. And when she shakes her head, I pop it into my mouth, because after this shit night, I'm low on fuel too.

Systematically, I put together various combinations of the different offerings and line them up on the edge of the desk where Truie can see them. The first to spark interest is a candied pecan—a single fucking nut that she takes way too fucking long to eat. She's probably expending more energy nibbling at her choice than it's providing. No wonder she's light as a fucking bird.

Next is an apple with the smallest slice of brie possible. Each time I find something she likes, I assemble two more, not that it makes any difference. Total, she might consume less than a handful of food before her interest lags, and if her slow even breaths are anything to go by, she succumbs to asleep. Barley enough to keep her alive. So, I add *Have a conversation with Winnie* to my neverending to-do list.

There's no doubt that Truie's a mess, there never has been. At least not since she was found. Before that, she was a powerhouse. Small but mighty. I saw her stand watch when Winnie's parents sent her to do their dirty work. Watched Truie stare down the dumb shits who thought they were getting more than what they were offered. She was strong when Winnie was weak and took care of her friend. Winnie let it spill that they were prepared to leave town, just now, but back then too.

Then Truie was grabbed.

She was held, hidden away for months.

She endured some vile fucking things at the hand of the man who died tonight, not to mention the men he allowed free rein.

And when she was found? Well, she was a ghost of her former self, and I need to get her back.

Chapter 7

Twisted

TEAGUE

"Why the fuck didn't you tell me any of this shit?"

My boss is officially delusional.

"You specifically said not to disturb you under any circumstances. Did that once last night and didn't really love the outcome, you know what I mean?" I turn the computer monitor my way to check on Truie.

Christophe spins it right back so he can watch Winnie.

I flick through the screens on my phone until I find her. I need to know there're eyes on my little hummingbird and there's no chance she can just fly away.

"Lapin cleaned up last night?"

"That's what Eddie said."

The man himself waltzes in and sprawls in the chair next to me. "She did. Nice and tidy. Pretty sure she reduced the traceable body count by at least half. What the fuck went down last night?"

"You really want to know?" I ask, knowing full well his answer.

"For the love of God, no. No details."

"But—"

"Nothing I don't need to know, you know the deal."

We do. We're well versed in only telling him the parts he needs to do his job, and he does it well, so... there's no need to fuck with a solid system.

"Alain thought he could take what's mine. That's no longer his position," Christophe says flatly.

"No. That's currently flat on his back at the morgue, isn't it?" Both hands push the iron-black locks back to the base of Eddie's skull, gathering them into an efficient tail. He winds a band around it two times, then a third. Then he leans back and folds his hands placing them low in his lap.

Christophe's mask of indifference breaks, his mouth tipping up on one side as he lazily lifts a shoulder.

"What'd he say about the file before the blade in his neck made talking an issue?" Eddie ignores the phone buzzing in his pocket and stares at Christophe expectantly.

"What do you mean? He was shot."

The other men share a look like they're in on some secret that I'm not privy to.

Eddie's gaze slides to me while he maintains his physical focus on Christophe. He dips his chin saying simply, "He was."

I check the CCTV on my phone and then hold it face down on my thigh, my leg bouncing. Unlike Eddie, I hate not having all the details. "That didn't kill him? He was sprawled in his chair, he looked lifeless. There was blood everywhere."

"Most of that was superficial," Christophe explains. "The mysterious *unnamed* shooter clipped him, sure, but most of that blood was from shattered glass. The bastard used Winnie to pull himself back to his feet and then had the fucking nerve to try to leave with her." His gaze flicks to Eddie before he shrugs nonchalantly and continues, keeping his recounting of events as generic as possible. "He was an old man, not in very good shape, you know? I had no idea that his balance was so bad—maybe he had some vertigo? But apparently, he fell down the stairs. Tragically, he ended up with my father's blade protruding from his neck."

Eddie purses his lips and nods. "Now that we have that ironed out—"

"Nothing is fucking ironed," I tell him before turning to Christophe. "And your father's knife? Neither of you think that's going to be a problem?" I should be glad to have the focus at least partially off of Truie, but holes don't magically appear in the abdomens of stabbing victims. She's not off the chopping block yet.

"The knife was never recovered after Alexandre's death. Obviously the wrong man was framed, blah blah blah, and the real killer came back to hit Alain. Again, we're good. Moving on." Eddie pulls his tablet from his bag and consults his notes there. Must be nice to be so fucking sure of shit.

"Jesus, Alain had his brother killed—"

"But Alain did not do the actual deed. That man wouldn't get his hands dirty when there are so many others willing to do that shit for him—"

"To save their own ass," Christophe finishes the line of thought. "Which brings us back to the file, right?"

"So it would seem."

Christ. What the actual fuck with these two?

"And that's it? Just... that's..." I raise my hands, in the universal *what the fuck* gesture, knee still bouncing, energy spinning, and my phone goes flying. It lands screen side up between my chair and Eddie's. He swoops down and picks it up before I have a chance. "Give it." I sound like a fucking kid on the school grounds who wants his toy back.

He tips the screen toward him, and in the brief flash I have of it, I can see Truie sitting up in my bed staring at the camera. The thin t-shirt she has on is over-sized but twisted tight and hides nothing.

I shoot to my feet and swipe the phone from his grasp, pocketing it.

"Look at you, not telling me more than the absolute minimum." Eddie chuckles. That in itself is a rare occurrence, but man, now is not the time.

"Fuck off, you ass." I tag my laptop from the edge of Christophe's desk and stalk across the room toward the door. "I told you everything I know."

"You mean everything you think I need to know." Eddie's voice is flat.

I pause in the doorway, turning to stare him down. "Yeah, I do. You're the one moving the bar, playing the game but constantly fucking with the rules. So yes. I've shared what I think you need to know to look out for us and for what's ours. When you figure out what you want to share about this book—file—then you let me know. Sooner is better." I throw his words back at him and storm through the lower level of the mansion until I'm inside my suite.

Pissed off and snarling is not the way I want to enter my bedroom, though. Fuck knows, I'll scare the life out of Truie. The only reason I left her to meet with Christophe and Eddie is because she was out cold and I had eyes on her.

At that thought, I pull my phone out and disable the cameras in my suite. Security doesn't need to have access if I'm here. I take a breath, and then another, forcing a calm into my raging body. I need to find some semblance of control before I cross this room and open my bedroom door… and I really want to open my door.

I want to rush in and scoop her up, check every inch of her to make sure she's okay, and then do it again to actually convince myself. But I lean against the closed door and wait until I'm no longer feeling like I could bounce out of my skin.

Eyes closed, my shoulders relax in incremental bits with each measured breath. Jesus, chilling the fuck out is harder work than I'd like to admit. And it's boring. Silent.

Honestly, it's unnerving not having my eyes opened wide, taking in everything around me and processing it, filing it away for when I might need it. I feel exposed. Vulnerable. And I fucking hate it.

A noise far too close for my comfort has me pushing off the door, fully aware. My fists clench until they hurt.

I'm halfway across the room before the source of the quietly rustling footsteps registers.

Truie stands before me, her tiny frame swallowed by my shirt, her hands stretched out in front of her, defensive and trembling.

I take another step toward her but pull up short when she retreats out of reach. I hold as still as possible, not an easy task for me, and match my breathing to hers. One breath turns into two. Each of the next is more controlled than the one before, longer in and slower to release.

For Truie, I can do breathwork. For her, I can force myself to be still. I can grasp hold of all the control in the world and give it up just for her.

"Little hummingbird." I say, my voice low and steady. A shiver runs through her. The fact I can see it is testament that she needs more peace in her life. And that I need to buy thicker shirts because her sweet little tits shook with that shudder, her nipples bunched into hard little peaks.

God help me, I want to wrap my lips around the tight pinched buds and suck them in, nibble on them, and see just how hard I can make them. See if she can come just from that. Drop to my knees and taste her. Make her come on my mouth. To see her completely undone, replete with pleasure.

I swallow hard and shove that shit deep down where it's safe. I don't want to scare her. And when the time comes and I do give over control to her, I'm desperate for her not to be scared of me.

So for now, I try to keep things light. "Did you have a good rest? You slept? Do you feel better?" Each question is accompanied with a sweep of her features, a check in with the pulse that flutters in her neck.

Moments pass before I get a small nod, and I match it, putting everything I have into making her feel safe and calm.

"Are you hungry?" That's met with the smallest lift of a shoulder and the way that acquiescence feels like the biggest win is insane. "How about a smoothie? Something sweet for you?"

At that, her eyes light up, and she rolls her lips between her teeth. God, she almost looks excited at the prospect of a fucking smoothie.

I pull my phone and tap a message to the kitchen staff requesting a pineapple-banana smoothie with an extra scoop of protein powder for her and my usual chocolate and peanut butter for me.

"Garrick should be here with those shortly. You want to curl up in front of the fire while we wait?" I ask the question, but I'm already moving toward the fireplace to stack wood and light the kindling. When the flame is solidly established, I slide my suit coat off and fold it over the back of the sofa.

The oversized chair is angled the way it has been since I learned that Truie enjoys a cozy chair, a throw blanket, and a roaring fire. I drop into it to take my shoes off. As quietly as can be, she approaches, perching on the edge of the cushion closest to the warmth.

I shift, making room for her, but also ensure that my body is between hers and the door. Nothing and nobody will get to Truie again without going through me. Literally, if that necessity presents itself.

I wedge myself into the corner, and Truie pushes back, sinking further into the down-filled cushions. She startles when the door opens moments later, admitting Garrick, two smoothies on his ever-present tray.

He hands Truie hers, before tagging the gray knit throw from beneath my suit coat and carefully draping it over her legs. Only when she's completely taken care of does he hand my smoothie to me. He ducks out the door without a word, leaving us in silence.

I'm learning to love the silence. It's not natural for me. I grew up with more cousins than I could count and fell into the chaos of Christophe's world without hesitation. The only time I've welcomed silence and stillness is with Truie.

So, we sit in the quiet while bedlam rages outside the nest we've built for ourselves.

I watch in wild fascination as she sips at what amounts to a liquid meal, wrapping her lips around the straw, cheeks hollowing out, and the heat from the fire painting her skin in a rosy glow. I fight the flow of want and need that has my smoothie forgotten and my dick getting hard.

Chapter 8

Suffocating

TRUIE

I WOULD LOVE TO CLAIM I'M GETTING BETTER, THAT things are settling, and I'm able to let in the light. But each instance of peace is fleeting at best, bracketed with feeling out of control and moments of full-blown panic.

I know some time has passed since I killed Alain. And I'm aware that I've spent almost all of that time in Teague's suite. After sneaking out and following him down the hall, seeing yet another monster from the depths of my own personal hell, I've been more than good with staying right here.

I'm happy, if you can call it that, when Winnie comes to spend time with me.

And I'm safe when Teague is nestled here in the

chair by the fireplace, laptop open on the arm of the chair or balanced on his knees as his fingers fly across the keyboard.

Generally, I'm as okay as I think I can be in the light.

It's when the darkness closes in on me that I struggle. When I've slept hard and gotten lost in the dreams of *then*.

Back then, I was strong. I worked out, danced, and ran. I was so, so very capable.

In the *before* times, I watched Winnie's back, made sure she was covered. In the after, she's been my literal savior. I would be dead without her, and would've ended all of this suffering well before now.

And now…? Now I have to figure out what to do.

How to live without her watching over me.

How to be strong again when all I want to do is crumble.

The comfort I felt yesterday is still here.

I assume it was yesterday, though I could be wrong. Time has a way of scrambling for me, like the abstract concept goes even further sideways while twisting and twirling, weaving its way into a fabric that can be so fucking terrifying.

The haze of memories—of the times when I thought I was such a little badass, that nothing and no one could touch me—flickers, dancing just on the edge of consciousness. And that, my friends, is by design. Because reality is too much for me to process. Where I am now— broken and hiding in the dark, compared to the bright and shining light of past-me—is enough to send someone much, much stronger into a tailspin. A deep dive into depression and anxiety... and hopelessness.

Yeah, I can't do that again. I survived it once— survived a lot of shit once upon a time—I can't do it again.

I inhale deeply and burrow further into the welcoming comfort of this bed. The scent is warm and delicious. The subtle weight of my covers is perfect, the heft and the bulk of it soothing like a hug. Neither too much, nor too light leaving me feeling exposed or like I could float away.

The bed beneath my cheek moves at the same time I register a low, masculine rumble echoing from the same place. Fear shoots straight down my spine, skittering along every nerve ending and through every muscle fiber, freezing me where I lie.

My breath is so shallow, I would almost guarantee it doesn't look like I'm breathing at all. I slit one eye open and then the other, finding a vast plane of white cotton that was probably crisp and perfectly pressed several hours ago. It likely didn't have a damp spot of drool right below my mouth either, but here I am.

"You're awake." The words echo through me, deep and comforting, beneath my cheek.

A hand, massive and full of restrained power, slides up my spine and wraps around the nape of my neck, capturing me. Holding me firmly in place. Trapping me.

Panic crashes into me like a rogue wave, threatening to pull me under and strip me of all control. Every muscle pulls taut. My lungs cannot suck in air, and my brain just fucking stops functioning. It stops.

I'm nothing but a ball of terror, traumatized by vacant, distant memories. Drowning in a flood of abuse and torture and pain. So much pain. Dear God, when will this ever end? I'm so tired of the constant oscillation of emotions.

"No, darling. *Shhh...* None of that now. You're safe, remember? You're safe with me; I'm not about letting anything happen to you."

Words are just words. They're weapons used to manipulate and scar. I've heard those very promises repeated time and time again until believing them was easier than remembering who and where I was. Because losing myself, disassociating from what I was experiencing, was the only way to get through it.

And the where? Yeah, I didn't want to think about

where I was held. Or about who put me there. Certainly not about all the things they took from me.

But this voice is different. It's the one from my dreams, soft and lyrical. It's not associated with my nightmares.

"I've got you, love. Nothing is going to happen to you. *Shhh...* Let's get you breathing, yeah? With me now, in—there you go—and out. Good girl, again. In and out."

Something inside me shifts. Only slightly, barely even worth noting, but it does. A loosening in my chest, in the muscles that were squeezing the air from my body. Enough for me to follow along with this voice and take the smallest breath—inhaling and then allowing an exhale.

Inhale.

And out again.

Each cycle I go through is rewarded with more murmured encouragement. Praise for doing the simplest, most basic of life-supporting tasks. And the voice that carries those words to me is low and sure. Like the deepest darkest crimson velvet, soft and plush. Warm and rich. It softens my sharp edges and wraps me in something that feels so foreign I know I should be terrified.

But each word uttered, every phrase whispered to the crown of my head, has me opening up further.

Breathing deeper. Inhaling and exhaling like I'm a fucking professional, when I've gotten way too comfortable with holding my breath instead.

Physical awareness comes back to me in dribbles and bits. The suffocating grip on the back of my neck is gone, but the firm solid weight in the shape of an impossibly large hand rests against my back. Holding me securely but not pinning me down.

Fabric rustles, releasing a warm, fresh waft of... What is that scent? Fresh cut grass and sunshine? I settle even further, burrowing my face into the solid wall beneath me. Broad planes of cotton-covered muscle, with the perfect dip for me to hide away from the world.

How is it that this feels safe? God, how is it that I can even pretend to know what safe feels like? Since the day I was taken, safety has been nothing but an illusion, a foreign ideal that was meant for other people, not me.

Hard as Winnie tried, even she never quite got that feeling down with me. But this?—whatever this is with Teague—seems to have imbued security right into my skin. Tattooed it on me like an indelible mark. And that has me completely off-kilter.

"Look at you."

"So brave."

"What a good job you're doing."

"Absolutely stellar."

"Fucking brilliant, you are."

Each phrase is mumbled, words sifting through my hair, across my brow, against my temple.

And little by little, the tension that flooded my system with adrenaline begins to dissipate, until I fully recognize where I am.

And who I'm with.

I lift my head and meet his gaze. Soft brown eyes, half-hidden by low, lazy lids. Freckles dot his cheeks; the soft cinnamon flecks a sharp contrast to cheekbones carved of pale granite.

I want to touch them, connect them, dot-to-dot, and trace his masculine beauty with my fingertips. I want to map the lines between fierce predator and the soft man who whispered all those encouragements during my freak out. During *this* freak out and the rest, because there have been many.

My gaze drifts down over his strong, slightly crooked nose to his lips. There's a freckle there, perched on the line of his lip that's shaped like heart that has melted in the sun. Golden stubble dusts his cheeks and chin, trailing down his neck. He's always clean-shaven, but the sleepy eyes and stubble might be my favorite version of him.

The top few buttons of his shirt are unfastened revealing... revealing... God, how can a throat be so alluring? The dip in the center of his collarbones, the lightly sloped planes of his pecs, the shadow of lined ink pressing through the opacity of his dress shirt.

Before I can overthink what I'm doing, I push at the linen revealing the fine detailing of a Celtic cross over his heart. I trace its lines. I can't help myself... the artistry is beautiful. If he inked it over his heart, it must hold special meaning to him.

The shirt falls away as Teague unfastens button after button. I wait for fear to wash over me, but all that shows itself is anticipation—and not the bad kind.

Not dread. Not terror. No trepidation.

The lack of negative feelings is almost unnerving to me. I want to see more, touch more. I want to explore him, tracing each ridge and dipping my fingertips into every furrow, to follow the lines and see where they take me.

"You're concentrating pretty hard there." His voice surprises but doesn't startle. There's no harshness, no ire, just a gentle observation.

I don't react other than a small shudder that skates down my spine. My words are so, so untrustworthy, and I don't want to get caught in the loop of them, tripped up by sounds that come hard, if they come at all.

Instead, I reach out and show him what's swirling through my brain. I touch him, trail my fingers over the spots that intrigue me, circle his nipple with my nail, captivated when it goes tight.

Teague groans, low and deep within his chest, as if he's fighting to keep it contained. As my fingers drift and explore, I catalogue each delicious response, a groan, a sigh, the tightening of muscles, and when I trail a fingertip lightly along the side of his ribcage, he squirms, pulling away from my touch and gives me the sweetest, almost boyish giggle.

My gaze snaps to his.

His face is magical. Eyes bright and bracketed by lines as his cheeks are pushed high with his smile. Straight white teeth flash, framed by lush pink lips, the look teetering between flirty and feral.

I stare, trying to make sense of what *I'm* feeling because I'm not as scared as I think I should be. I know far better than anyone that if I play with a tiger, I should expect to be bitten. But I don't think Teague will bite me. I don't think he's scary. I don't think he's cruel or mean or evil. At least not to me.

"What are you thinking, hummingbird? What's got that curious little brain of your all atwitter?"

"T-twitter?" I laugh at the absurdity of this man with the broad muscles and deep voice using such a silly word, all while the way his accent curls around the syllables has the muscles deep in my belly pulling tight.

"Mm. You like that? The way I say *atwitter*? What else might I say that you'd enjoy?" His gaze takes a leisurely assessment, touching on each of my features, lingering on my mouth before settling on my eyes and staying there. I'm almost squirming by the time he whispers, "*Is tú mo ghrá geal.*"

My breath catches in my lungs, and my heart stills before trying to break free. "What d-does that m-mean?"

"You are my shining love. My bright love."

"That-that's... It doesn't make me laugh," I say unnecessarily. It's stupidly obvious to both of us that I'm not laughing.

"Ah, but did you enjoy it?" Teague's gaze dips back to my mouth as if he needs my response so badly, he wants to see it and experience it, not just hear the words.

"I, um, I d-don't think it f-f-fits."

He moves slowly, placing his hand on the side of my neck, his thumb sliding back and forth across my lower lip. His eyes are molten pools of milk chocolate that I would gladly drown in. "Hummingbird, there is nothing more fitting."

Chapter 9

Ruined

TEAGUE

I stare into her eyes, my gaze bouncing back and forth, left to right. How does she not see her own brightness? How does she not see the way she brings light into a room, that it glows around her like a halo? That she is the embodiment of light itself...

My muscles tighten under her touch as I crunch up to press my lips against hers. They're soft, incredibly soft, and supple. Everything I imagined.

Everything I hoped wouldn't be true.

Because now that I've tasted her, I don't ever want to let her go. Not that that was ever really an option anyway. Being in the next room, the suite across the hall, the office on the other side of the house is way too far. Letting her go? Yeah, not happening.

I tease the seam of her lips and suck on her lower lip. When I nibble, sinking my teeth into the tender flesh, she gasps the sweetest sigh. And that's my in. I sweep my tongue inside her mouth and drink her in.

She's fucking delicious. Addicting. And I want more.

I frame her face in my palms, then slide one behind her head and angle her so I can deepen the kiss.

She's hesitant, almost clumsy in the way she kisses me back, her fingers pressing hard against my pecs. Tension. There's tension in the way she's holding herself above me.

I back off, slowing the kiss before pulling back to check in on her. "Are you okay?"

Truie's eyes are dazed, not with fear but maybe... maybe something better. She nods slowly, her hands finally relaxing, her shoulders becoming more pliant. "I'm, um... Yes?"

She bounces on my chest as it rumbles with my chuckle.

"You don't sound sure."

"I'm n-not. Not really." Her curls tumble, framing her face in a pale cloud. A bright cloud.

She's not frozen in fear, not trembling. Her eyes

aren't vacant. All good signs, but I want to give her a minute to see if any of that changes. So, I bring us back to before I rocked my fucking world with tasting her. It's probably not a bad idea to calm myself as well.

"Then answer my question, what had your cheeks lifting in laughter? What had you staring so intently at me?"

She searches the space just to the left of where my head rests against the headboard, like she has to sift through memories to find the answers. "You... You laughed. You're ticklish?"

"I am. Terribly so." I reach for her hand and move it back to my pec and hold it there, almost positive she won't slide it down across my ribs to the exact spot that holds my secret. There are precious few people who know I'll crumble into a giggling mess if properly tickled. "What else? You were thinking of something big before I giggled."

"You did giggle." She's so wildly amused by that. "I was thinking... I... You're k-k-kind."

Her words hit me square across the chin like a sharp jab. And maybe her tone is what does even more damage. Like being kind is an anomaly. "Does that surprise you?"

She tilts her head and stares at me for so long it's almost uncomfortable. I don't push her for an explanation, no matter how badly I want to. Prying words from Truie is a futile pursuit.

When she finally speaks, that jab delivers a knockout blow. "Why w-wouldn't it surprise me? K-kindness isn't a given and I"—she pauses, seeming to count through her breath—"I know better than to assume."

Oh my fuck, that slays me. Absolutely slays me. Not willing to release her hand, I slide my free one to the back of her head, twining my fingers through her messy curls. "I've tried to be mindful of that. I don't want to scare you." I search her eyes for any hint of distrust, glad when I don't see it.

"You're n-not that way with...with everyone, though, are you?"

I hesitate to answer that directly, so I make her a promise that I hope she believes. "I will never be anything but with you." I kiss her softly, trying to convey the sincerity of my vow.

Truie melts into me, her hands soft as they roam tentatively along my skin. I shift her fully onto my chest and allow my hands to take in her petite frame. She's so small, so slight, that my hands completely span her spine when stacked, from the dip of her neck to the curve of her ass.

The way I want to cup her and move her should be

illegal. It would take nothing to shift her down my body, line her up with my aching cock, and thrust against her.

Truie starts to move as she takes control and deepens our kiss. She rocks her hips, rubbing her sweet little clit against my abdomen.

My hands fall naturally to her ass, encouraging her as she chases her pleasure. I release her when her movements stutter at the added pressure and dance a light touch up her back, caressing her silky skin beneath the oversized t-shirt. The material shifts, exposing her to the cool air. Goosebumps rise and another shudder goes through her.

"Okay?"

Her *yes* is nothing more than the hint of a whisper that skates along my neck as her soft lips make contact again.

I shove my head against the headboard, arching my back so I can lie flat and give Truie access to all of me. Thankful that movement doesn't scare her, I allow my hands to roam elsewhere.

Her knees are hiked high on my ribs as she straddles me, and I glide my hands along the thin cotton of her leggings.

I want to rip them off, toss the shirt she always seems to find to the ground, and roll her to her back. I want her splayed out for me, spread wide for me to taste and tease, to kiss and lick and suck leaving tiny red marks on her skin to show she's mine. Marks that no one else will see, because if they did, I'd have to rip their eyes from their heads. Fuck, I'd have no choice but to kill them because there's no way I could stand them even having that memory.

I test the limits of touch, backing away when she stiffens, revisiting those spots to see if the reaction changes.

Her shirt bunches between us, the bulky fabric pushing us apart. Any barrier, any distance, is too much. I slide my hands up her ribs, noting the definite lack of ticklishness.

"Can I?" I push at the gray cotton, and Truie goes completely still. "No is a complete sentence, hummingbird. I'm not going to fight you on that, not ever. If you're not comfortable with something, you tell me, and I stop. No question. No explanation."

As is her way, she pauses, gathering her thoughts, taming her words. But then she surprises me sitting up straight and slipping her arms from the sleeves of what has become her favorite t-shirt. Slowly, the fabric lifts.

With painful patience, she exposes her flat belly, the ribs that hold her precious strength within. The bottom curve of her tits are just about my undoing. Gorgeous in every way and tipped with tight rosy nipples. Every inch of her is nothing short of perfection, but when she pulls free of the shirt, her wild curls are backlit by the light from the sitting room, glowing like a halo on the angel that she is.

My heart stops. My breath stalls in my lungs, and I swear I've died and gone to Heaven. But I'm fairly certain that I'll not be granted entry to that particular kingdom, so this must be Hell. Tempted with Truie, but unable to touch her.

Her arms drop, crossing over her exposed breasts, and her eyes shutter. "I'm s-s-sorry. I, um..."

"Absolutely not, love. You have nothing to apologize for. It's just harder than I'd imagined holding myself back. To not roll you to your back and ravage you. I'm fairly certain I'm not worthy of looking at you, let alone touching you. Christ, I'm trying so hard. I don't want to scare you."

"I... I'm not. Scared, I'm not scared. Not with you, and I..." Pause. Count. Inhale. "I don't know what to do with that. Not being scared kind of...scares me."

I wrap my hands around her, resting them gently on her hips. Fingers splayed, thumbs perched on the crease of her thighs. "I don't want you scared in any way."

She pushes at where my dress shirt clings to my shoulders, like the fact that it's there is a problem.

I knife up, sliding her off my abdomen and to my lap

as I do. My shirt is on the floor in record time, and Truie's lips are parted in a surprised O.

"I thought you wanted that gone?" She did, right? I didn't imagine her pushing at the fabric? Almost scowling at the mere presence of the linen?

Her hips roll and shift, and I realize it's my dick that's the issue here. Fucking hell. "I'm sorry. I can't make that go away quite as easily, but—"

Her mouth crashes against mine, silencing the offer that might have been the death of me.

Truie kisses me, all traces of shyness gone. She rocks her hips, undulating against my cock, and if I'm not careful, I'm going to blow in my pants. It's been ages since I've done that.

I think of horrible things, the heinous things I've done, to ward off my release, and let her have free rein.

"Christ, you're mesmerizing," I murmur as she swivels and bears down.

Frustration pinches her features, and her movements turn jerky, frantic.

I slide my hands down over the curve of her ass, palms firmly planted on the warm skin beneath the fucking leggings that taunt me on a regular basis. I push at them, exposing her backside, shove at them until they're banded around her upper thighs.

The world stops.

Everything stops.

Truie fucking stops.

I pull back but don't let her go. Not that I wouldn't, that she can't get away from me if she needs to... But right now, it feels like if I let go, I'll lose her forever.

Her hands push between us and drop to the exposed skin on her thighs. She's covering up, hiding herself from me.

"What?" I ask, probably more harshly than necessary.

Truie shakes her head, her kiss-swollen lips pressed into a tight line.

I soften my voice, dropping it low and ask again, "What is it, hummingbird? What did I do?"

I don't want to lose her eyes, that connection is far too important right now, but the urge to see what she's trying to cover is really fucking strong.

I stroke her thigh with my thumb, brushing against where her hands press frantically to her skin.

I steal a glance and trace the raised ridges of dozens, maybe hundreds of tiny scars lined up like soldiers or tally marks decorating her perfect skin. I saw them when I pulled her from where she was held captive. Saw the fresh marks, the stain of blood, but how they were carved into her skin is still a mystery.

"Truie, tell me the story of this." With gentle prodding I nudge her hand to expose the marks more clearly. She shakes her head, looking on the verge of tears. "Safe, remember? You're safe with me."

"They're gross. It's…"

"Nothing about you is gross, love. Did you do this? Was it a way to control when you couldn't?" Conversation now is a challenge. Back then it was impossible.

Her eyes close, and her shoulders rise, tension lodging where it'd previously been gone.

"You can tell me anything. I will never judge. Nothing you say can change the way I see you."

This pause is longer than the others and that makes perfect sense. She's either shutting down or gearing up to tell me something wildly personal and painful.

Minutes pass, and I don't break contact through any of it, instead stroking the tiny scars that stripe her pale, creamy skin. Feeling the sharp lines of them against the pad of my thumb and cataloguing them as best I can.

"Th-th-that was what he used to d-d-do." Her stutter blooms, catching her words and threatening to hold them hostage. But Truie is far too strong to allow that to dim her.

Pause.

Count.

Breathe.

"When he came to see me, he-he would bring a blade. A razor. He like the blood. He ruined me."

She crumbles into my chest and hides her face as tears pool then run down my pecs between us.

"You're not ruined. You are not broken. You survived something that was absolutely shit, hummingbird. You're perfect just the way you are."

She's killing me, this girl.

Chapter 10

Shudder

TRUIE

I am so fucking tired of this. So tired.

I never thought I'd be interested in sex again, let alone feel my belly tighten with desire.

I didn't think I'd be capable of wanting someone, of allowing myself to be vulnerable in the way that being naked in front of another person requires. That I could feel the promise of an orgasm build and begin to coil, winding me tight.

And, just like that, the brakes were stomped, and all the bad shit came roiling back up to the surface.

So fucking tired of this.

I don't even know where my mind was. The only

thing going through my head was how strong Teague is. How safe I feel with him. How normal it all was.

I felt good for the first time in a stupid long time. Very good. Better than I'd ever felt. Because, in my vast sexual experience, I've never had an orgasm.

My encounters have been limited to a single instance of fumbling teenage sex in the backseat of his mom's car where he got off and I had to question whether it even counted, and traumatic, often violent rape. It was rape. Every time and in every way, it was rape.

So, so tired.

But this? Today? With Teague? This was different.

And I ruined it.

I mean, how do I come back from a near breakdown over the scars covering my thighs? Because forcible sex wasn't enough for the bastards who had me at their mercy, so they left behind permanent reminders of the havoc they wreaked. Fine ridges, almost like a barcode in some places. In others, the lines are a random crisscross from different days, different moods. Always the same man.

Strong arms wrap me in a tight embrace, grounding me instead of caging me. "Hummingbird, you cry for as long as you need to, wash that shit away. But don't shed tears for my sake. What happened is in the past, you had no say in what was done to you. When you're ready, if you want, we'll find someone to help you work through it all."

For some wild reason, that is the tipping point. But instead of allowing the dark to take me, drag me to its depths, and swallow me up, I laugh. It's really small, that first laugh. Really small. And I think it shocks both of us, because it's Teague who goes stock-still, not me.

"Can you tell me why we're laughing? And is this just a you thing or am I supposed to be finding this funny as well?"

With the way he goes rigid, I know he's pulled back enough that he can see me. He's waiting for a sign, permission, maybe for the bottom to drop out and for me to completely lose it.

At this point, anything's possible, but weirdly, I think I'm okay-ish.

I'm mostly naked, my soul laid almost as bare as my ass, orgasm failed, and leaking tears all over the man I literally thought was just a dream. Yay, me.

As my body expands, my lungs filling completely, the steely arms surrounding me remain steady.

"You can laugh if you want." I stay where I am, face pressed against Teague's chest and glance to the side hoping my discarded shirt is within reach.

"What do you need? You're after something."

This just keeps getting better. If I were still wearing a shirt, I'd tuck my face inside and wipe away the tears and snot. But past-me was feeling all kinds of confident, and a certain kind of way, and tossed that balled-up, baby-soft cotton across the bed. Shit shit shit.

"I need a tissue," I reply, my voice muffled against him.

"A what, now?"

"A tissue. My face is a mess and—"

"It's absolutely not." Teague releases his hold on me and places a hand on either side of my face, tipping my head so he can see me. His thumbs swipe at my cheeks, but there's no hiding my red blotchy face and swollen eyes. "You're perfect."

"You keep saying that, but..." My words trail off as he shakes his head, denying that there is a *but*.

"Perfect."

He waits for my protest, but I'm struck silent at the sincerity in his eyes.

He waits for me to pull away, to hide, but I'm held captive in the way he's supporting me.

He waits for me to fall apart, but this time, I don't want to.

I want to be better, stronger. I want to take back control, whatever that looks like. I want to make my own choices and write a different ending to my story.

To do that, I lunge wildly to the side, making a mad grab for his dress shirt, and use it to wipe my face clean of snot and tears. No matter what this man claims, snot is definitely not perfect.

He laughs. Not as big as when I tickled him, but still a good laugh. "Feel better?"

"I really do." I match the grin on his face with my own.

"Can I kiss you?"

I shake my head. "No. I think I'd like to kiss you, if that's okay."

"Anything you want," he whispers, leaning close. He stops just shy of pressing his lips to mine, giving me agency over what happens next.

We share the same air for the beat of my heart, and then I close the distance between us and kiss him. I kiss him. I sweep my tongue out, and he opens eagerly. I tilt his head, the way he did to me, angling for better access.

Teague gives over control, but I feel clumsy instead of empowered, and frustration creeps in.

"If... What if I don't actually want to be the one driving this? What if I want you to... to take? To be in charge of everything?"

"Anything you want, remember?" He slides his hands until he's palming my neck instead of my cheeks.

"But you're still in control. I won't take anything from you. I'll only give."

And just like that, the desire I felt earlier coils in my belly. "I don't know how that works. I only know—"

"Mm, we're going to change what you know. Expand your knowledge and give you new experiences that will replace those shitty ones, yeah?"

"Okay?"

"Anything you don't like, that you're not comfortable with, you tell me. Is *stop* a word that gives you trouble?"

I shake my head, and he continues, "Good. Then say stop, and I will. If, in the moment, even that word fails you, use your other faculties. Push me, tap me, kick if that's what you need, but I promise you, I won't let it get to that, okay?"

"Okay," I say, surer this time.

With that, Teague lays me on the bed, gently. Carefully. He kisses me until I'm breathless, trailing kisses and nibbles and little licks down my neck.

His eyes meet mine, waiting for consent before he slides down my body and cups my breasts, plumping them, teasing my nipples. He flicks them with his thumb until they're tight buds, standing erect, and begging for attention.

He licks and sucks first one and then the other, and my belly swirls with desire. Every move he makes, each flick of his tongue is with permission and patience.

His patience, because I'm becoming increasingly impatient. I want more. Need more, but I don't know how to convey that.

"Anything you want," he mumbles around the nipple in his mouth before biting down gently.

My hips roll at the sensation searching for the feeling, that friction, I had before falling apart. Rocking against his belly and then his hard cock was... That's what I want. I want that coil, the curling and tightening deep inside me. I want the release that was just beyond my reach.

The temptation is strong to back away, to pretend that this is all I want, that it's good enough. But it's not. And Teague knows that.

His hand slides down my stomach, settling between my legs. My leggings are still on, but awkwardly so, rolled and bunched low on my hips. He strokes me, slowly, deliberately, concentrating on the spots that illicit a moan or a sigh, circling my clit through the thin fabric.

It's just not quite enough. I squirm, frustration threatening again.

"Tell me what you need." Teague's breath is hot as he leans impossibly close to my pussy. He slides his hands beneath my ass and buries his face between my thighs, inhaling deeply. "Fucking hell, I want to taste you."

Once again, his gaze flicks to mine for assent before he continues narrating all the things he wants to do, his finger tracing the path, marking each spot. "I want to slide my tongue the length of you, lick your cunt from bottom to top, suck on your sweet clit until you shudder and shake. I want to fuck you with my tongue and drink you up when you come all over it. I want to give you an earth-shattering orgasm that takes your breath away, leaves you pliant and satisfied."

I push my fingers through his dark auburn waves and say the word that manages not to fail me in this critical fucking moment, because I can't not come again. Not tonight, not with the filthy, beautiful words still hanging heavy in the air.

"Yes," I whisper. Barely a word, it's more of a sigh.

Teague stares up the length of my body, his eyes locked on mine.

I nod, and he curls his fingers around the waistband of my leggings and pulls them free. As my scars are revealed, he presses his lips to kiss and worship them.

A shiver rolls through me as he sucks a particular messy cross hatch into his mouth. He releases me with a pop and his mouth is right there. *Right there.*

He flattens his tongue and drags it along the seam of

my pussy. My back arches at the intimate contact, and I moan, the sound so foreign to my ears, I clap a hand over my mouth.

He reaches up and wraps his hand around my wrist, tugging that hand free of my mouth. "Please don't keep your sounds from me. I want to hear you. Every sigh, every moan. Please, hummingbird, I want them all."

He places my hand low on my belly and holds it there beneath his own.

"Can I?"

Whatever the specifics, it does not matter to me in the slightest. I give him another *yes* and another and another and another as he licks me and kisses me and sucks on my clit, just like he said, coiling me tighter and coaxing me higher until the wild sensations are just too much.

And on a moan that would be so unbelievably embarrassing if I could find a fuck to give in this moment, I come undone.

Chapter 11

Balls

TEAGUE

My balls are officially disgusted with me, and I'm over my cousin showing his face around here.

Desmond has come to the house one too many times for my liking, unannounced. Sniffing around, looking for information I'm not about to give him, asking pointed questions about who's currently in the house, how many guests we have in for Alain's funeral, and if any of them are a young woman with pale, white-blonde curls.

None of which he really needs to know. Heads are going to roll for the simple fact that he even suspects she's here. And how could he?

The cameras at Alain's were thoroughly wiped the night he stole Christophe's woman and found himself stiff and cold, including those covering the exterior. Though the asshole who failed to make that happen until after he was reminded, is no longer doing that job. Or much of anything... But what's one more body for Lapin to take care of?

If only my cousin was as easy to delete.

I check our security feed to confirm that Desmond is off the property and at least pointed back toward town. We need to add more cameras on the lane, maybe tap into more of the ones in town so I can keep a better eye on that asshole. I don't need him surprising us again.

As I make my way back to my suite, I run into Winnie strolling along like she doesn't have a care in the world. It wasn't that long ago that she was locked in a guest suite as part of Christophe's scheme to take back control of his father's empire, only allowed in the hallways if she was properly escorted. Other than the time she tried to steal her best friend out from under my nose and escape. Not that I would have ever let that happen.

Now Winnie's traipsing through the mansion unaccompanied.

Eh, not really. She's got a guard on her at all times, but now it's more to protect her than to keep her caged. And when he's not trailing her, he or Christophe are watching closely as she moves from one CCTV camera to the next.

"She's doing well today," she tells me as we pass. "She ate almost a whole bowl of soup."

A fucking bowl of soup.

It's something, but not enough.

"That much? Really? She better watch out or she'll get an ass on her." As soon as the words are out of my mouth, I want to kick myself. I have no right to say shit like that. "Sorry. That was—"

"Rude. But I get it. She's too thin. She needs"—Winnie looks up at the ceiling, blinking rapidly. When she meets my gaze, her eyes are glassy and sad. "Tru needs to heal. To talk to a therapist, work through everything that happened to her. She needs to get away from here. Be somewhere safe for a change."

Ouch.

The words hurt, but that doesn't discount the truth in them. And if I'm honest, those are all things I want for Truie too. I probably need to bring it up again when she's not naked in my arms. Half naked, I completed the job after offering her a therapist. I blame my disgruntled balls for fumbling that.

I turn and continue on, retracing her steps. "I'll see what I can do."

The scoff behind me isn't subtle, and neither is the muttered, "Asshole." But what stops me in my tracks is when Winnie adds, "She's stronger than she remembers.

She deserves revenge for the things she lived through, *that's* hers to take."

I face Truie's best friend, the woman who has tended and cared for her since she's been back. "She got her revenge when she shot the miserable piece of shit who stole her away. What she needs to find now is peace. Because with peace, comes power and *that* is what Truie needs full ownership of."

Winnie is silent as I close the distance between me and the object of my... What is she? My focus? Absolutely. A distraction? That too, but she's more. Always more for me.

Before I press my palm to the scanner, I count to five, schooling my features, relaxing my shoulders. A handful of rounds of controlled breathing would be great, too, but I don't want to take the time. I need to see her, to see for myself that she ate that whole bowl of soup, that she's here, and safe, and whole—as whole as she can be.

The mechanism hums, granting me access, and there she is. Tucked into the corner of the chair, the fire crackling, and a bright red throw blanket held firmly in her hands.

"Hey. You get to spend some time with Winnie?" Sure I know the answer, but it's a question Truie can answer in a myriad of ways, and how she responds will tell me so much more than the answer itself.

Her eyes turn in my direction before her head pivots, but they're bright, open. Almost in the neighborhood of happy.

"I did." She takes her time with each of the two simple words, and the result is spectacular. No stuttering. No tripping.

I rest my hand lightly on her shoulder, contact but not intrusively so, and take in the empty bowl but full plate.

"Looks like the soup was good today. Didn't like the sandwich?" According to Winnie, it's one of Truie's favorites—grilled turkey and cheese on sourdough.

The shoulder beneath my hand rises, barely. The movement is so slight, I might not have noticed if my hand wasn't right there.

I feel useless.

My skills for fixing shit seem to be lacking when it comes to Truie Cochonette.

Sometimes it just clicks and I know exactly what to do, what to say. And then there's moments like this, where I stumble over myself and everything feels like the wrong thing.

"Is there something different you'd like?" Because I

will deliver no matter what her request. I have no problem sending Garrick out for whatever might put a smile on Truie's face.

"I..." The implied *never mind* is nothing more than a shake of her head, platinum curls bouncing free as she rolls her lips between her teeth.

"Do you need time to think? Or are you afraid to ask?" I round the back of the sofa, pulling my suit coat off and depositing it on the back of a straight uncomfortable chair before settling in next to Truie.

The grilled sandwich is cold now, but I'm starving and not about to let it go to waste. With the plate balanced on my thigh, I shove half the sandwich in my mouth and chew. The action makes it less obvious that I'm going to sit in silence and let Truie answer my question. Sometimes, it takes longer for her to work out what she wants to say and whether she really wants to say it or not.

Sometimes it's like she's shocked by her surroundings and seeing me throws her off.

But the silence isn't awkward. It never is with us which is weird for me. With anyone else, any other time, silence would feel oppressive and I'd have to fight the overwhelming need to fill it.

My phone vibrates in my pocket once, then twice,

then a flurry of messages bombard me, shaking the plate that teeters precariously on top of it.

Obviously, I need to see what the hell is so urgent, but when Truie makes another attempt to tell me what she wants, nothing else matters.

"I want"—a pause full of determination—"something sweet." No stutter. A drawn-out S in *sweet*, but discounting that, she asked for something. Truie fucking asked for something, and now I will move Heaven and Earth to get whatever she wants.

"You want one of your smoothies? Candy? Ice cream? Gelato? Some cake?" Each offering of a sweet treat is punctuated with another rattle of the plate. Much as I want to give her my complete focus, I have got to see whose world is imploding.

I set the plate back on the table and pull my phone from my pocket, thumbing the screen to life. Notification after notification after mother-fucking notification is stacked on the screen and every single one of them are from Christophe or Eddie. The last one turns my blood to ice.

> C: Put the hummingbird in a glass house. D is on his way back to cage her.

Me: Done.

I don't bother looking at the rest of the messages, there'll be time for that once Truie's safe. The challenge now is getting her out of here without panic and sending her back into her own personal Hell.

Sadness shrouds her eyes and even as she darts them away, I can see that I've missed something important. Important to her at the very least and really, that's what matters.

"I'm sorry, shouldn't have gotten distracted. What is it that you've decided on?"

She doesn't look at me while shaking her head, the avoidance amplifying the disappointment I feel in myself.

"Tell me," I prompt, because time is getting tight. We need to go.

Her tongue darts out and slicks her lower lip. Nervous? Indecisive? The why matters, but the act itself is distracting as fuck, and I have to remind my balls they're not in charge and shove down the urge to follow the trail her tongue makes with my own.

This is so not the time for that. Again, there will be time for that later. I can be a patient man when I want.

"Gelato. I want, um, gelato." Her brows are pushed together, and her hands twist the throw blanket as she pulls it closer, almost like a shield. "It's okay though. I d-don't n-need it." The head shaking is back and, if I had to guess, I'd put the cause with getting stuck on those couple of words more than the idea of not getting what she wants.

I push to my feet and hold my hand out to her. "I beg to differ. You absolutely need gelato. Let's get your shoes and a jacket." I want to reach for her, rush her out the door and down the hallway to my Range Rover. I want to spirit her away from here, hide her away from the vile piece of shit who thinks he can just waltz in here and take her away from me.

Instead, I pull a *fuck no* and pack her up on the guise of getting her something sweet. I will without a doubt make sure she has her gelato, but we're not coming back here. I'm going to have to send for more of her clothes, have Garrick pack them up and deliver them.

Jesus Christ, and I'm going to need a change in job titles, there's no way to do the shit Christophe needs from me. It's not like my work translates well to the whole work-from-home model. I'll have to figure that out later too.

That fucking to-do list for *later* is growing longer by the minute.

"Ready for an adventure, hummingbird?"

Truie freezes, holding tight to the hem of the sweatshirt she just pulled over her head. It's one of mine, an old one from college, soft and worn and fucking perfect on her.

I've loved seeing the way she clings to my clothes, opting to use my wool coat in lieu of a blanket, sometimes choosing my lounge pants over the soft pastel leggings I had brought in for her. My shirts. My socks. There are times when I scoop her up at the end of the day to tuck her into bed, that I find one of my white undershirts clutched in her hands beneath whatever blanket I've managed to swap out for my coat. The soft cashmere knit has to feel better against her porcelain skin.

"Just to get gelato, and maybe a drive? You've been stuck here for a long time, change of scenery might be good." It's a lie wrapped up in tiny truths, and I fucking hate the dichotomy.

A lot has happened since the last time I tried to spirit her away from the estate. Hell, both times I've had her in the car with me have been nothing short of disastrous, but I need her safe. And at the moment, this place doesn't qualify.

Slower than I care for, she acquiesces, slipping her hand into mine and following me through the halls.

I open the passenger door and help her into her seat. Her reaction when I put my hands on her is better and better every time. Mine though? Each touch is harder on me than the last and I have to work at thinking boner-killing thoughts.

Sure, I gave her a mind-blowing orgasm, but when she shared that it was her first?—yeah, we'll be taking shit slow.

After everything she endured, I can't imagine she'll be comfortable with me grabbing her ass and rubbing my dick all over her any time soon. I want to wrap my body around her, cover her in tender kisses and some not so tender ones. Explore every sacred inch of her.

"Can you manage your seatbelt, or do you need my help?"

"I can get it." I know she can. Each jump in her confidence brings her back a little bit more even if it steals an opportunity for me to touch her in the short term.

I round the SUV and climb behind the wheel, pride fighting with desire. I blame my balls.

The need to touch her is overwhelming, so instead of relying on the camera display, I sling my arm across the back of the passenger seat, turn my body, and reverse out of my spot.

Then I let my hand linger.

A touch of her hair becomes a perfect silken curl spiraled around my finger. A brush of her shoulder becomes a caress of her delicate neck. A slide down her arm becomes her hand clasped in mine.

And Truie doesn't pull away. Her delicate hand, smooth and cool, stays in mine, and I revel in that win. I also resist the urge to put it on my dick. Go me.

The drive is quiet and comfortable, though the creamery in town is seasonal and most definitely closed this time of year. Not that showing our faces in town was really on the agenda anyway.

Truie registers the fact that we're not headed to town and the same time I hit the turn for the thruway. "We're not going to town."

"No." I take a chance and lift her fingers to my lips to soften the blow.

"It's closed?" Disappointment laces her question.

Did I know that before promising? I totally did, but it was the perfect excuse to get her in the car without scaring the shit out of her.

No need for both of us to be shaking in our shoes.

"Mm. I've got a better idea," I offer.

With a quick pulse of her hand, I glance over to check her reaction. It's not horrible, so I drop the bomb and pray there's no explosion.

"I have gelato at home."

"Then why did we leave?"

I love that she's comfortable questioning me. And I

hate that the *not horrible* reaction might just go to shit now.

"Not at the mansion, at my home." The rising tension is still within the parameters of *not horrible* so I keep going. "I had the drive fixed since last time. There's a small area of gravel, just to maintain the anonymity of the place, but beyond that it's been paved."

The gravel drive was an issue last time I tried to take her to my house. It set off an avalanche of emotions that had her spiraling. And when I tried to leave her there, safely tucked away, she lost her fucking mind. I showed back up in Christophe's office looking like I'd been through hell and back.

Twice.

Truie's eyes dart side to side, her jaw tenses, and those luscious lips I can't seem to stop thinking about going flat, thin. But she doesn't pull her hand from mine, so I stroke my thumb across her knuckles and slide our hands to my thigh—not my dick. I should get a fucking award for the restraint I'm sporting.

She does her thing—pause, count, breathe, and finally says, "Okay."

"Okay?" I could kick myself for questioning her, but I'm not going to lie, I'm a little surprised she agreed so easily.

"Yes. Okay. I"—she shifts in the passenger seat, sitting just a little bit taller—"I'll be okay this time."

"And if I have to leave?"

"I won't… I won't f-fall apart. I promise."

My heart bottoms out at that, like she's already apologizing for shit she has no idea about.

Chapter 12

Negative

TRUIE

I do a lot of positive self-talk, hyping myself up on the drive.

I feel a little like I got tricked into this adventure in the name of gelato. But tension has been high at the estate since I shot Alain. And I'm doing better than I was before. Kind of.

Teague stops the car in front of his gorgeous mountain home—mansion is more like it, but it's rugged in a sleek, refined way.

I'm excited to see it again, through different eyes. Maybe we'll stay for a while this time instead of a trauma drive along a gravel lane that went on forever and a day that was supposed to end with leaving me here alone.

The resultant panic attack was exhausting. Not doing that again. No way, no how.

He steps out and rounds the SUV, opens my door, and offers his hand to help me out. But my God, the excitement rolling through me is way too much for anything so staid.

I don't know if I fall into him, or catapult myself from the vehicle, but my senses take their leave. Hell, they do a serious disappearing act because my feet are dangling well above the ground as he clutches me to him. Silent laughter rumbles through his chest and small puffs of warm air ruffle the hair against my neck.

We're pressed together.

He's holding me close.

And I'm okay.

Embarrassment heats my cheeks, and all the doubt and discomfort come rolling back in. No... not discomfort, Disbelief, maybe? Definitely self-consciousness.

I unwind my arms from around his neck and place my palms high on his chest. With as tightly as he's holding me, it's the best I can do.

"I... I'm sorry. I, um, I... I..."

"Don't. You're perfect, Truie. I'll tell you that until you believe it."

When I brave a glance at Teague's face, a small grin

pulls at the corners of his mouth, and his eyes are creased with fine lines.

Beneath the tips of my fingers, the ridge of his collarbones gives way to the dip of relief below. I touch and press, exploring the different sensations. Bone and muscle covered by cotton and wool.

Teague murmurs, "Hummingbird," low and full of gravel.

Air seizes in my lungs, and I jerk my hands away, balling them into fists and pressing them to my cheeks. Gravity catches up with me and before I'm ready, my feet are back on the ground. The space between us swirls with cold, cold air.

Fucking awkward. I'm so fucking awkward since... *then*. I stare straight ahead, letting my eyes go unfocused on the dark gray wool of his coat. Shit. Shit, shit, shit.

Warm palms cup either side of my face. "Hummingbird, come back to me. Don't let the darkness take you, we have gelato to eat. We have shit to celebrate, yeah?" The smallest bit of pressure has my gaze lifting to meet the warm dark pools of his irises.

"I'm sorry." I try to shake my head, but he holds me fast. I don't like being restrained like this, but the fact that Teague doesn't let me run and hide from him is not as bad as it could be. I think I might like that he does this. Like maybe I'm important enough for him to hold onto. *Maybe.*

"No apologies. Come, I have blackberry, lemon, and hibiscus sorbet and chocolate and coffee gelato. And, darlin', we don't need to choose. They're all here just for you."

The inside of the house is more magnificent than I remember. Last time I was here I was in the throes of a full-on freak-out from sensory overload. The only thing that could have made that worse is if I were closed inside the trunk of a car.

Gleaming wood and stacked stone contrast with black granite and stainless steel. Deep leather sofas face each other flanking a floor-to-ceiling fireplace with green velvet chairs angled cozily in a nook by a wall of windows. I want to sit by a roaring fire with my gelato—or maybe the sorbet—or curl up in one of those chairs, a mug of tea between my palms, Teague's wool coat draped across my lap.

It's cozy without feeling closed in.

Dishes clink on the counter, spoons clattering next, and then tub after carton after container of delicious, sweet, icy promise.

"Mind dishing it out while I get a fire started?" Teague asks. Already striding toward the back door, he leaves me unattended in the kitchen.

Outside, Teague piles split logs into one arm, loading more and more. More than I'd think possible, more than maybe necessary. Just more.

He pushes back inside, locking the door behind him, and takes in the fact that I haven't moved a muscle. But he doesn't stop. Doesn't cater to me or berate me or even scowl. He just notices and then goes about unloading the wood from his arms into a copper trough beside of the mantle.

He sheds his jacket, tossing the dark wool across a chair so casually, like it doesn't matter at all.

I stare at it a moment, tempted by the warmth it holds from his body, the scent of him imbued into the wool, held there for me. But then... Jesus, he crouches down on his haunches and with all the surety and confidence I only wish I had, he lays the fire. He's patient with the small spark, coaxing it into flame. Feeding it, nurturing it until the flames dance and the fire roars.

Seemingly satisfied, Teague stands, hands on his hips, and assesses his work.

The finely knit wool of his sweater stretches across the broad expanse of his shoulders, tapering down to a narrow waist. His forearms, exposed by the sleeves he pushed up and a single roll of his cuffs, should be illegal. They taunt and tease and have the audacity to end at those strong hands, thumbs framing the curve of his ass.

I'm completely and utterly engrossed when the low huff of a laugh catches me, red-cheeked and staring.

"You okay there, hummingbird?"

I melt. I die. I curl in on myself and go completely still.

"Uh uh. Don't do that, I'm just checking on you." He drops his hands and turns toward me, a handful of long strides bringing him right in front of me. His gaze darts to the countertop where he laid out everything we need, and the bowls still sit empty. "Smart."

I scrunch my face in question, not at all willing to test the word gods right now.

"Giving the gelato and sorbet time to soften. Good plan. Chocolate gelato and black berry sorbet sounds like a good combo, yeah?" He reaches up, smoothing the valley between my brows with his thumb. "I can't wait to see what you choose for yourself." He steps away then, disappearing deeper into the house.

I stand motionless, dumbstruck and frozen, waiting for him to come back. I wait for the angry words, for the scolding, the strike that always seemed to accompany my trauma, giving it form and shape. Substance.

But none of that comes.

Why can't I just be a normal human being with normal reactions? And just be *normal*?

Normal would be dishing up our desserts. So, I take

a step, and then another until I'm right there, scooping frozen treats into bowls like a regular, non-traumatized *normal* person.

Each scoop of chocolate and blackberry are perfectly symmetrical and fill the bowl, the spoon tucked carefully to the side. The other bowl holds a small taste of each of the sorbets.

I roll my lips between my teeth and glance at the hallway Teague disappeared down.

He should be back now, shouldn't he?

I wait, counting to sixty and do it again. When I've completed a third round, I squeeze my hands into tight, tight fists and release them, and set about closing each of the containers and tucking them back into the freezer. See? Normal.

The door closes on a nearly silent *whoosh* and I jump, my heart stuttering to a momentary halt as the low rumbled words found me.

"That's not nearly enough."

I cringe, breaking as I apologize. "I-I'm sorry." My hands shake as I open the freezer and reach for Teague's flavors.

"Oh, hummingbird, no. I have plenty, but you need more. In fact..." His words stop as he reaches around me, plucking the remaining sorbet flavors from the shelf with one hand and tucking the gelato away with the other.

His free hand drops to my waist pulling me out of the way of the closing freezer door. My back pressed against his front. The tip of his thumb so close to the underside of my breast, only just barely not skimming it.

And it's all so... natural. Normal.

Until it's not. Until I pull in a sharp gasp, breaking the moment.

Fingers press into my belly, lips to the top of my head. "You're okay, Truie. You're perfectly safe."

I want to believe him. I really do, but trust is so damn hard for me. So hard. I know I've come a long way in a really short amount of time and that I attribute to Teague. To his kind heart, his protective nature. His patience with me. Always so patient and understanding.

For fuck's sake, he saw my scars. Didn't freak out at the sight of them, or worse, add to them. No, instead, he gave me a freaking orgasm.

When I finally can, I nod, but Teague steps away from me. He fills my bowl with almost as much as his, tucks the containers away, and grabs our dishes, stepping around me to sit in front of the fire, on the floor with his feet extended toward the flames.

"Come join me."

I do.

Teague devours his gelato while stealing a bite of my sorbet here and there, all the while talking. Soft words about nothing and everything. Lingering touches and small casual caresses. Always talking, filling the space that I can't.

When our bowls are empty, Teague sets them both on the coffee table behind us.

His hand finds mine, and he holds it like a cherished treasure.

The fire has light dancing across his face, fighting with the shadows.

"I have a confession." The way he says it is solemn, quiet. Almost reverent like he's seeing absolution. "I knew the shop was closed. I brought you here on purpose."

There it is—confirmation that this trip is not the innocent *oops* he tried to portray. "D-did you?"

"Ah, I did. I'll not apologize though." The slight lilt that is usually just part of his regular speech dips deeper, grows stronger. "I've told you you're safe with me, always, and I'm not a liar."

"Okay?"

"Somehow, the police department is under the impression that you're to blame for the death of Alain Robicheaux. They want to bring you in, interview you. Likely charge you with the crime and lock you away."

I sit there, silent, because what can I say? I shot the man, and he died. He deserved much, much worse.

"The officer... he's dirty. Been paid for years from Alain's accounts, and now, obviously, his paycheck is threatened."

"He c-came to the house. After." If it's *him*, the same cop, he won't stop. He'll never stop. He'll hunt me down and cut me again, hurt me over and over again until he gets what he wants.

This nightmare is never going to end. I don't know what I did to deserve this hell, but I got it. I would love to unsubscribe to this part of my life, but I don't think I can. I think this is all I'm going to know for the rest of my life.

Fear.

Panic.

Darkness. That darkness is closing in again.

Soothing sounds sift through my haze, bringing me back again.

"*Shh*, don't let it win. You're stronger than you know, and I promise you're safe. I won't let him take you, hummingbird? That's why I brought you here, so Des can't get to you."

Despite his assurances, the tears come, streaming down my cheeks and dripping from my chin.

Teague releases my hand and wraps his arms around me, pulling me into his lap. He cradles my head to his chest, and I let the tears flow. Soaking his sweater and probably the shirt beneath.

I lose myself to my tears, to the fear of being at Desmond's mercy again. I can't do it.

Soothing hands stroke down my back, my arms, grounding me. Keeping me from losing myself completely.

Murmured assurances and the way they rumble beneath my cheek lull me to sleep.

Hours later, I wake, hot and disoriented. I turn my head into the pillow and wipe the drool from my lips.

"Mm. Thought maybe you'd plant a kiss over my heart, not drool all over it again." Teague's voice is low and laced with gravel. "Though I don't think I'll complain about be being drooled over."

He sifts his fingers through my hair, pushing it back from my face as embarrassment wraps her prickly fingers around the back of my neck.

"What woke you, darlin'? It's still the middle of the night."

I feel dry, wrung out from crying. "Where are we?"

"In bed. You cried yourself out and fell asleep in front of the fire. When my ass fell asleep, I carried you up." He presses his head into the pillow to better meet my gaze. "You wouldn't let go. Clung to me, actually."

That tracks since I'm currently sprawled across his chest, hands fisted in his sweater. I loosen my grasp, one hand and then the other, placing my palms flat on his chest. I should move. Slide off of him and give him space, but his hand is firm on my lower back, holding me in place.

The dark room is lit only by the full moon glowing brightly above the trees. Washed in a photographic negative, Teague is a contrast of light and shadow. Silver and smoke. The sharp lines of his cheekbones, the bump on the bridge of his nose, his eyes—all brought into stark relief with the play of light.

His lips look ripe and soft. Luscious and right there for the taking.

I've spent a lot of time staring at that mouth, memorizing the shape of those lips, dreaming of what they taste like, wondering if they're kind or if the teeth they cover are full of venom.

I do know they're capable of making me forget.

"Truie, darlin', you tryin' to kill me?"

Chapter 13

Contradiction

TEAGUE

The way she's staring at my lips is fast becoming a problem.

I'm damn proud of my control, the restraint I've managed with Truie should be celebrated in the streets. Honestly, I should be fucking commended. Win a prize.

My eyes are heavy lidded as I stare down where she's splayed across my chest, at the only prize I'm interested in.

This sweet fragile thing has clung to me since we arrived at the estate. Found comfort in me like she *knows* me. Like she somehow recognizes who it was that carried her limp and broken body out of that dungeon of hell.

There's no way she can actually know it was me, that

we met well before I escorted her out of that cemetery, and I knew her well before she was taken. Tru's been in my life way longer than she knows.

"Truie, darlin', you tryin' to kill me?"

I don't get a response, at least not a verbal one. No, the little hummingbird perched on my chest rolls her plump pink lips between her teeth, her perfect little tongue peeking out to swipe along them until they're glossy and wet.

She shifts off of me, and I immediately feel the loss of her. Her warmth, her fragile weight. Her breath skating along my neck.

I reach up and drag my thumb down the corner of her mouth, not to clear away any remaining drool—no, I just want to touch her lips, but I know I still need to proceed with caution.

"You're hot. You don't have a fever, do you?" I reach for the lamp at the side of the bed filling our little corner of the room in a soft glow. I run the backs of my fingers along her cheeks, her forehead. While she's warm, she's not actually feverish. Though the gorgeous pink flush painting the apples of those cheeks is telling some kind of a story.

"Just warm." Two simple words, but when she pushes back, her ass to her heels, and pulls the hoodie she's stolen from me over her head leaving her in a snug tank top, I want to believe she's saying so much more.

She picks at the bottom of my sweater, running her finger beneath the cashmere, and stops just shy of where the hem is rucked up, untucked from my trousers.

Timid and terrified, yet bold and brave. This woman is an utter contradiction and absolute shit at the subtle art of seduction. She's clumsy with it, not that there's a need to be anything different. She's the perfect mix of sin and seduction without even trying.

"You should, um…" She forgoes words and slides my sweater up my torso looking a little lost when it's gone as far as it can with me flat on my back.

So, I sit up and reach behind my head and grab the soft material between my shoulder blades and pull it off.

My dress shirt is a wrinkled mess and feels too fucking tight, like a straitjacket. I want to whip it off too, but I don't want to be the one pushing. I hold my breath and count to calm myself.

When I hit ten, her hands are sliding toward me once again. Twenty has her reaching for the third button, the top two already undone. Thirty has her working her way down the placket, releasing each button until she hits my navel.

I want to grip the sides and rip it the rest of the way open, scatter the buttons to fuck knows where.

But I wait. I wait until her eyes meet mine again, pupils wide, questioning. I wait until she slides her palms up my sides, skating over my ribs and fisting the linen. She tugs it off of my shoulders and discards it to the side of the bed.

"Hummingbird, what are you doin'?" I search her eyes for an answer, but she just shakes her head.

"I... I..." she pauses, takes a deep breath and slowly blows it out through pursed lips.

I don't push. I don't prod or try to hurry her words. Despite the huge strides Truie has made opening up to me, none of that will do us any good. When the pressure is on, she shuts down.

So, I wait. Because I never thought I'd actually be here, with her taking initiative. That this would be happening again and not a one-time thing. Not in a million years. I've hoped for it. Imagined it. Stroked myself to the thought of her touching me, sucking me, bouncing on my cock. But those were just abstracts.

My body is perfectly still, almost rigid... Well, part of me is very rigid. Stiff. Turgid. Engorged. That should go without a doubt, but the rest of me is hanging by a thread.

I'm afraid to close my eyes in case this is just a dream. Terrified to move a muscle or to reach out and drag her to me. I don't want my barely contained lust interpreted as aggression. If I scare her? Throw her into a memory of...*then?*

Nope. I couldn't live with that. So, I lay perfectly still and let Truie touch me.

First, it's a single finger drawing a straight line down my chest. Then a second finger joins in the exploration with a third hovering, dipping to skim my pec, my nipple—that sets my skin on fire.

"Talk to me, hummingbird. Tell me what's going on in that beautiful mind."

The trail of her touch slows and pauses, as she lifts her gaze to meet mine, as if her exploration can't continue without both senses working together.

"I don't want to go with..." She stalls like saying his name might conjure him.

"Desmond?" I get a nod, but it's accompanied by a shiver, and not a good one. "Yeah, I don't want that either. That's why I brought you here. No one knows about this cabin, no one but Christophe and Garrick." I hoist a brow when her lips quirk up into a grin. "What?"

The attempt she makes at hiding that grin is cute, pursed lips have dimples popping in both cheeks. "It's not... You can't call this a cabin. It's m-much too big." She's not wrong. "But you'll stay here with me? You won't leave?"

God, if it were only that simple. And there I go

again, wishing I had a normal job so I could work from home and spend every possible minute with her. But if my job were normal, I never would have found her. Not initially when I was looking out for Winnie, and not when I carried her out of that dungeon.

"As much as I can, but there's gonna be times I have to go to the estate, do things that can't be taken care of from here."

The skittishness that's always lurking has abated, though for how long, I have no idea. But for now, I give in to the urge to touch Truie, to assure her that everything will be okay. That I won't allow anything bad to happen to her. I wrap my hand around hers and hold it against my chest.

"And I'll go with you, right? To the estate? I can see Winnie and—"

I hate cutting her off, but... "No. Not now, not yet. You're safest here."

"I'm safest with you," she insists, the little furrow between her brows deepening.

I fucking wish. Nothing about the current situation is good. How did we go from Truie stripping off our clothes and touching me, to the very conversation I brought her out here for—and avoided because of her fears?

"You're safest here. Out there, at the estate, there are

too many eyes, too many people watching us, seeing you. Too many people who have access to you. And if that gets back to Des, he'll... Fuck, it won't be good." I cup her cheek with my free hand and wait for her eyes. Only when I've got them locked on mine, do I continue. "I will not let him take you, hear me? I'd have to be dead and buried for that bastard to lay a finger on you, let alone take you away from me, and even then, I'd find you."

"You can't promise that." Curls bounce wildly as she shakes the thought away. "You can't...you can't know that."

This is not how I planned to broach this with her. It was supposed to be a conversation in the light of day, over breakfast, maybe. Or after I had her good and relaxed, pliant from orgasm after orgasm after orgasm.

"Oh, hummingbird, but I can."

She turns her head, shaking off my hold, and pulls at her hand I have clasped to my heart. I hold tight as she demands, "How?"

"You trust me?"

I wait and get a tilt of her head. That's it. I don't blame her for being wary, but this is me. The person who carried her out of Hell. The one who watched out for her before she was taken, who searched for her once she was gone.

"I know it's hard, Truie, but I need your words.

I've kept you safe, yeah? Made sure that you're comfortable, that you have what you need, what you want?"

The muscles in her jaw tic as she clenches. When I think her teeth will crack if she doesn't let up, she finally acquiesces. "Yes. I trust you."

My eyes fall shut as I release the breath that I've held hostage for way too long and when I open them again, she's right there, staring at me. Not avoiding me anymore but pinning me in place and holding me accountable.

"I have a little chip. I could place it under your skin and then, if I have to leave, I can track you, always know where you are."

"Like a dog. You…you want to chip me like a dog." She blinks at me, slow and steady. "You've got to be fucking kidding me."

"I'm not. Dead serious." I reach toward the nightstand and pull my phone from the charger. When the app opens, I turn the screen to show her. "The app would allow me to see where you are at all times."

"Like a fucking dog," she shouts. Not even a hint of a stutter there.

This has gone so far off the rails, I'm not sure how to get us back on track or if the train is even going in the right direction. It feels like the engine has run away and is crashing off the side of a bridge, plummeting into the river of fire below.

I jackknife up to sitting, the move far too sudden, and Truie startles. "No. If I'd done this before, had this in place when Alain's men took you, they never would've had the chance to lay a finger on you. I'd have cut them off, killed every single one of them. I failed you then, I will not fail you again."

"You...? If... Failed me? H-how could you fail me if you didn't even know me? That happened before... I don't understand."

Moving slower now, cautiously, I cup her face between my palms. Her brows are pinched together over wide glistening eyes that shred my heart to pieces. There's so much she doesn't know because while she was there physically, she wasn't really *there*.

"You feel safe with me because you recognize me, your heart recognizes mine, Truie.

"I've worked for Christophe for a long time." I soften my features, praying she can find it in her to forgive me. At least accept what I have to tell her. "Winnie was my mark, my job. I watched her, helped her for years when Christophe couldn't be seen in town. It was a job I wanted to hate, that I should've resented, but I couldn't because it brought me to you. Your strength, the way you watched out for your friend, and stood up to anyone who tried to take advantage of her… Do you remember when she started taking on drops for her father? I was there, watching you watch out for her. God, you were such a little badass, leaning against your piece of shit car, arms folded across your chest as you stared down some of the shittiest people in this town.

"Somewhere along the way, you carved out a place in my heart. You rooted your way under my skin and became a piece of me. And it killed me when you went missing. Then seeing you, battered and broken, bloodied on that concrete floor in the dark? Fucking killed me." I hold her close, gaze bouncing between her eyes. "And I refuse to allow that to happen again. I cannot lose you a second time."

She fills her lungs and holds the air as if letting it out again would be giving up control, allowing a wall around her to crack, and letting the darkness to seep through the fissures.

Chapter 14

Uncaged

TRUIE

Then

My body is bruised and broken, but it will heal. Yes, there will be scars screaming to tell the story of pain and torture, of my trauma and survival. Sadly, I don't think strength gets a chapter in that story. Nor does defiance, because the fact that I'm still alive has nothing to do with me.

"Jesus, what did they do to you?" The voice is soft and lyrical, edged in disbelief and sharp with anger.

I don't respond. I can't.

If nothing else in the time since I was dragged in here, I've learned to keep my mouth shut and stay alert until it's time to disassociate. To remember voices, faces, and the touch that belongs to each of them.

And the pain of taking a simple breath after punishment for failing at those things rained down on me.

But this is a voice I'd like to remember.

Gentle hands lift me from the filthy concrete floor. Strong arms cradle me against the solid planes of a chest, wrapping me in a scent that I can't quite place. Warm and clean. Crisp and comforting—fresh like the sun. It mutes the pain that rips through my ribs.

I might be floating. For the first time since I was taken, I feel safe.

I feel hope, but hope is a dangerous thing.

I'd hoped to escape this town with my best friend and start over somewhere new with no history, no presumptions.

I'd hoped to be free and do something with my life that I could be proud of.

Hoped I could be safe.

But all of that was nothing more than a pipe dream, one that went up like smoke. Or like dust on a gravel road. I gave up on each of those hopes in bits and pieces. They were taken from me, extracted from me through hours upon hours of pain. Bled from me with every slice along my thighs, over and over and over again. Dripped and congealed, mixed with dirt and grime and things I didn't want to think about. Things I had to tuck away into a strong black box that I kept tucked far back in the recesses of my mind.

My mind. There's an entirely different kind of broken with that. One I'm not sure I'll ever be able to mend. Being awake, aware through all of the trauma that caused that rift... that's its own, never-ending kind of torture.

"What the fuck, Tig? Thought you said there were no survivors." The owner of those words sounds like he has a cold, nasally and whining.

"And that's the story we're going to stick with, yeah? No survivors." The arms holding me squeeze a little tighter and a whimper bursts free with the pressure on my ribs. "Goddammit, I need to get her out of here, have her looked at by a doctor."

A harsh laugh sounds from behind my back, and I push down the pain, swallowing another whimper. "I'd fucking love that. Think Doc can straighten out my nose? Not sure I like having it leaning so far to the left."

"Not my concern."

"Asshole." A loud clap follows the insult, and the man holding me jerks to the side. The movement jostles me sending more pain lancing through my body.

"Fucking touch me again, and it'll be the last time you're able, understand? The girl's injured far worse than your broken nose. Man up and get us out of here." Movement rocks me as my savior softens his hold, cradling me like I might break at any moment. "You all right, love? I've got you. We'll get you out of here, make sure you're safe, get you looked at and out of pain."

It's a promise filled with good intention. I totally get that. But pain is a necessity, not a nuisance. Pain lets me know I'm still alive. Sometimes it's the only thing I have to hold onto, to keep me grounded. It's precious to me.

"Nothing can hurt you now. I won't allow it." Then the voice drops lower, the lyrical tone strengthening. "Christ, you're nothing but a tiny little bird. Your pulse is fluttering like a hummingbird's wings." The soft words pause, and the chest I'm held against expands. It's solid, strong, and full of assurances. "I swear to you, I'll kill every one of them. Every man who laid a finger on you, who caused you harm, through word or touch, will die a painful death at my hand. I don't care how important they think they are, what kind of protection they think that have, I will slice them down. Fuck, I'll cut them apart, rip them limb from limb with my own hands. Still won't be enough, but they will never lay another finger on you."

This promise? This is one I can get behind. No one has ever offered me such a thoughtful gift before. Not even my own father. Certainly not when he sold me out to my captor.

He shifts me in his arms and, though I can't begin to think it's intentional after the vow that just spilled from his lips, pain stabs through my body, and the world goes dark.

When I come to the first time, the scent of sunshine and security is strong and solid against my body. A warm, calloused hand is hooked around my knee, a strong arm looped around my back.

"Don't you fucking stop this vehicle."

"They've got us caged in. We're either stopping or crashing," the driver grits out.

The chest I'm cradled against rumbles with a growl. "Just make sure you crash us through and keep going. We are not fucking stopping."

"But—"

"Just do it." Then, softer, lips pressed to my filthy hair, "Hold on, hummingbird. I'll keep you safe."

The engine revs.

Tires squeal.

Metal crunches.

And blackness takes me.

The second time consciousness finds me, I squeeze my eyes tightly closed, the light above me harsh and abrasive. Fingers skate down my left side, touching and pressing on my ribs as paper crinkles, sticking to my skin as I try to shift away. From the touch? From the pain? I'm not quite sure, but I'm caught in the chasm between staying perfectly still and clawing myself away.

The warm, solid wall of security has been replaced by a cold, unforgiving surface. The scent of sunshine and safety, overpowered by something sterile and antiseptic.

I don't like it.

I want to go back. Not to the dark, dank room filled with pain, but to the warmth. To the arms that held me close and sure.

"Pretty sure at least two ribs broken, not much I can do for those. Painkillers, rest, limited activity. The wounds, though. Where did you say you found her?"

It takes everything I have not to move, not to react,

not to scramble away. Instead, I keep my body motionless, stiff and awkward, making sure they don't know I'm awake.

"I didn't. Though I did tell you if you hurt her, I will do the same to you, ten times over."

The probing, painful touch stops leaving me breathless and floating until a warm hand envelops one of mine. The callouses dotting the palm rasp across my skin, and I calm just enough that my muscles stop pulling against my apparently broken ribs.

"I'll, uh... I'll be back in a minute with something for pain and the crap I need to clean up the rest of—"

The distinctive sound of a door closing cuts off the rest of the man's sentence followed by a huffed sigh.

The air in the room shifts, chaos and tension yield to calm.

"Promised to keep you safe, hummingbird. I always keep my promises." Soft lips brush against my knuckles with each word. "I know you're awake. Doc's going to give some medicine, clean your other...wounds. If he hurts you, you squeeze my hand, yeah?"

I count to ten, fifteen... At twenty-three, a thumb strokes the sensitive skin on the inside of my wrist.

"Give me a little squeeze so I know you've heard me." My finger twitches. "A little squeeze, love. Just a small press. I know you can do it."

The door opens, admitting the doctor.

I pinch my forefinger and thumb together, squeezing the hand of the man who keeps me from falling apart.

A low laugh turns to a rumbled growl as a needle is shoved into my ass cheek, and my pinch becomes a full clench.

"Fucking warned you about hurting her. That's one."

Light recedes from the edges of my vision, tunneling until the world goes dark.

The third time my eyes flutter open, the ground is moving beneath me, and I'm cradled in the strong arms once again. My head is heavy, the world around me fuzzy and hazy.

Each step brings new awareness to me. The warm, early summer air caressing my exposed legs. Soft, knit cotton covers my body like a dress. An awkward, too-big-but-doesn't-quite-fit-right dress.

I'm sore everywhere but able to discern between the new aches, like my ribs, and the old, well-established pain from where my body has been used and abused for weeks? Or has it been months?

I hope I never know.

I swallow down a groan, my breath catching deep in my lungs, putting pressure on my ribs.

"*Shhh*. We're almost there," my now favorite voice murmurs in my ear.

"Hurry up. We gotta get outta here, Tig." The nasal tinge is largely gone from the voice trailing behind us, but urgency is fully present in the whispered yell.

We stop and twist as my savior turns to address the man behind us. "Keep your voice down and get back to the fucking vehicle. I told you I don't need you for this."

"But—"

"Go. Follow my order and you'll see another day."

We continue forward, one silent step after another. A muffled *asshole* acting as punctuation to the previous statement.

I laugh, small and filled with pain that feels like a dagger to my side.

"Careful, hummingbird. I had to dole out justice to the last person who caused you pain, I don't want to have to go back on my promise. I will, though, because the only way I'm hurting you is over my dead body."

Every muscle in my body stills, except my heart which seems to take off on a wild sprint.

"Oh, hummingbird. Don't you dare worry, that's never going to happen. I've finally got you safe, I'm not fucking this up now."

Darkness lifts, and the air around us shifts, like we're stepping into the light. From the safety of cover, into a wide-open space.

"We're almost there, love, so I need you to listen carefully."

My hands rest on my stomach, soft and relaxed from the drugs or the trauma-induced nap I just had. I slide my left hand over my right and squeeze, hoping he sees the movement in the fading light and understands the unspoken agreement.

"Good girl. Your ribs are broken, your"—he pauses, throat clearing as if he needs to clear away emotion or gather courage—"your wounds have been cleaned and dressed as best as possible. I need to leave you for now, but I'm taking you to the only person I trust with your care."

Panic rockets through me, trembling shakes every part of me and pulls a whimper to the surface.

"Nuh uh, none of that. I may be leaving you for the time being, but I'm not abandoning you. There are things I have to do, take care of, and I can't do them if I'm worrying about you, yeah? Your friend will keep you safe. She'll take care of you, get you the help you need, and keep you safe until I can come back for you.

"I need to set you down on your feet, and I need you to stand for me until the door opens, okay?"

I squeeze my legs trying to trap his arm where it supports me, slide my hand to grasp at a shirt that is no longer there. My fingertips rake against the skin of his chest, gaining no purchase since my nails have been bitten or ripped down to nothing.

He drops his lips to my forehead, pressing courage and reassurance through the contact. "I'll keep you in my sights, love. Nothing and no one will ever hurt you again."

He sets me on my feet, a solid support at my back until I manage to find my balance. "There you are. I'm going to knock on the door and then I need to go. I promise not to leave until you're safely inside. Trust in me, hummingbird. Trust in me."

By the time the door opens, his warmth has leached from my skin, and he's nothing but a strong presence fading into the shadows.

My legs wobble, barely holding my weight, only to give out entirely, as recognition clears the haze of awareness surrounding me.

"Tru?" My name is a simple whisper of disbelief, and I crumble to the ground on Winnie's doorstep.

Chapter 15

Yours

TRUIE

T̲h̲e̲ ̲f̲u̲n̲n̲y̲ ̲t̲h̲i̲n̲g̲ ̲a̲b̲o̲u̲t̲ ̲p̲r̲o̲m̲i̲s̲e̲s̲ ̲i̲s̲ ̲s̲o̲m̲e̲t̲i̲m̲e̲s̲ they're kept. I mean, a lot of the time they're not, but when they are, it speaks volumes to the giver's character.

What's wild is when you've been through Hell and back, rescued from the depths, and have been hanging on to your sanity with the nubs of nails bitten down to the quick only to discover that the promise you've thought was nothing more than a dream, was in fact given freely and was wholly honored.

The voice from my dreams belongs to Teague.

The scent that has always inexplicably calmed me is his.

The kind man who held me so carefully, so reverently, is the man who feeds me sorbet.

Tig, who killed men to rescue me from a fate my father willingly bestowed upon me, who threatened anyone who caused me pain, is Teague, the man who has cared for me gently, softly, fully since the funeral for Winnie's parents.

"How…" I search for the question I want to ask first. There are so, so many rushing to the tip of my tongue, but I shove them down. I need to be careful, deliberate in how I approach the ever-expanding mountains of *hows* and *whys* so I don't send myself into a spiral of overwhelm.

"When I lived with the L'Oursons, after the hospital…" I shake my head as a different question forces itself to the surface. "The hospital? Therapy—did you…?"

"I didn't force it, but I made it possible for you to go for as long as I was able. I wanted you to get the help you needed."

"But…but… they pushed me out. Told me I was okay to leave. To go live my life and they put me out of my… my…my room?" My brain is making bets that my mouth can't quite cover, bringing my stutter up from the depths.

"And Winnie was there to take you home with her. She was there far quicker than made sense, yeah? One of the nurses called her to let her know and kept an eye on you until she arrived," Teague fills in for me.

There is nothing but sincerity painting his features, so I go back to my first question.

"Henri and Claudette never touched me. They didn't"—I swallow the urge to get caught on the consonants stacked together, controlling my breath until I can continue. "They let me be. Didn't push me into their stable, make me work at the Honey Pot to pay them for living there. Was that you?"

Teague rolls his bottom lip between his teeth and nods. "I made sure Henri knew farming you out was not an option. I watched him closely and made sure it was me who took care of his drops and exchanges for *les Milieu*. Every time he saw me, it served as a reminder not to test how deep my commitment to your safety ran. Winnie's too, but you became my paramount concern, and I made sure to stop by often."

His confession hits me like a freight train, and it takes a few quiet moments to absorb the impact. The beautiful thing is that he honors that and allows me to just...be. Even when I couldn't see him, didn't know he existed, he was looking out for me. That's a lot to take in. A lot to process. How many times was I upstairs in Winnie's room, hiding in the closet or in the corner behind her bed? And all that time, he was right there...

I stare at him, my gaze bouncing left and right, from one eye to the other, and pull in a lungful of air. *Jesus, he smells good.* And with that thought, I blink slowly, once and then again.

"Were you there? At-at Winnie's house? The day her parents died?" Could he be the one who killed them? I mean they were dancing with the devil well before then, but never that close.

His jaw works back and forth before he asks, "Did you see me?"

"I heard...heard voices. Heard... I don't know, it wasn't an argument, b-but none of the voices were Henri's or-or-or Claudette's." I search for some kind of a sign, a smirk, a nod, a twitch of his brow... I get nothing. He gives absolutely nothing away. "But I think I would remember if it were you. I think... I think..." Shit, I don't know what I think anymore. None of this makes sense.

"I was there twice that day," he admits carefully.

"Twice?"

"But I never said a word."

"Then how...? How... I feel like I knew. Like I recognized..." I shake my head trying to make sense of everything and I can't. It just doesn't want to come together for me, but this has happened to me a lot since I was taken. My brain fights me, doesn't always want to make the connections that are right there.

Frustrated, I drop my head to his chest, burrowing against his warm skin, and inhaling. I pray that something clicks. That just one of those little neurons will fire and give me what I need.

"Hummingbird?"

Recognition jerks me upright. "You were there," I say with more conviction than I've felt in a long time. "You *were* there. You... I..."

"You what?"

"Your cologne, I remember it. It was lingering, close to the foot of the stairs. That's why I didn't completely fall apart when I saw...saw that they were dead."

His chin dips, finally giving me the acknowledgment I've been searching for.

"I checked on them, saw that they weren't moving, that they were dead and then...and then...and then I"—realization slams through me—"I ran up to Winn's room, then back to the stairs. I sat on the landing and tried to breathe like they taught me in therapy. I stayed there where I could see them. I felt safest there."

"And is that where you stayed? Until Winnie came home? Until the police came and the bodies were taken?"

"No. God, no." The minute Winnie said she needed to call the police, I had to leave. I had to go to the woods, had to hide. Had to make sure no one found anything if they searched the house, so I went to the tree deep in the woods. "Did you kill them?"

"I did not. I had no reason to. They hadn't crossed me."

"But… Christophe? He killed Winnie's parents. And then paid for their funerals." A nod confirms both statements, so I continue. "And he took us from the cemetery?"

That one doesn't feel right, but I don't remember all the parts of what happened or the order of them.

"He took Winnie. I drove you in her car. You have to know that I hated calling Hibou, the doctor Christophe has on staff, hated that he sedated you, but I was worried. You shut down. I think I scared you and I hated that I was the one to cause you to crumble."

I shake my head, small tight movements. "You talked to me, wrapped me in your coat—your coat that smelled like you. You carried me, stayed with me until I fell asleep. You were there every time I needed you, every time I woke." My voice drops to barely a whisper, "And even when I slept. You stayed with me through all of it."

He huffs a small laugh, void of humor. "And the one time I left you alone, unattended, to take care of the bastard who was obsessed with hurting young girls, you stole away. Scared the shit out of me when I saw you on

Alain's lawn, gun in hand, wide-eyed and trembling. How did you even get there?"

"The door didn't shut all the way—just like after." He knows exactly what I'm referring to. "I heard guys talking, followed them through the woods and picked a gun from one of the bodies they left in a trail behind them."

"That was another failure on me."

"It wasn't a failure."

"It absolutely fucking was." I flinch at his tone, but Teague pushes on. "What if you'd been taken? Again, we're right back to my biggest fear, right? I can't live with myself if something happens to you."

"So you want to chip me—"

"Location tracker," he amends. "Fine, yes. I want to always know that I can find you, no matter what."

I think on that, turning his words over and over. It's not like I want to hide from Teague, I really don't. Maybe him having the ability to find me is a good thing. But I don't know that I can give up that kind of control without getting something in return.

"Will you get one too? Would you do the same for me?"

Teague stills. My question shocking him into...I don't know, a glitch? Is he buffering? "You want me to insert a tracker under my skin. Why?"

"Same reason." My confidence surprises me. "I want to know where you are."

"That's an occupational hazard, Truie. And how will you track me? Who will you tell? I don't think—"

"If you want to chip me, I get to do it right back to you. That's it. That's the only way I'll agree." My nostrils flair as I stare him down. "And I'll need a phone, with the app." This is a big ask, it wouldn't shock me if he laughed in my face and flat out refused.

But he doesn't. What he does instead is mutter low and under his breath, "Should have just done it while you were asleep. Asked forgiveness instead of permission." Then louder, staring deep into my eyes, he says, "Okay."

"Okay?" Surely it can't be that easy. This man, soft and caring to me, but a tiger not to be fucked with to the rest of the world, just agreed to allow me to put him on a leash? To always have my finger on the pulse of where he is.

"I told you, hummingbird, I'll do anything to keep you safe."

And there it is...

The promise made.

A promise honored.

And a promise kept.

"Is it..." My hands start to tremble. It's slight at first,

but as seconds tick by, the tremors increase in severity. "How do you do it? Is it going to hurt?"

Teague wraps his arms around me and pushes to standing, carrying me through the mansion he calls a cabin. He sets me down on the granite counter in the kitchen—the cold stone sending chills through my body—and pulls open a drawer to my left.

He rummages through the surprisingly normal chaos of a kitchen junk drawer, extracting a box of syringes and a handful of small packages. The drawer to my right holds more phones than a person could possibly need. And alcohol wipes. Which is decidedly not normal.

"You, um, you didn't answer me," I say, watching as he moves with frenetic efficiency, bouncing from one task to another and then back again to finish the first. He is chaos in motion. "Do you... Would it be better to finish one thing at a time?"

He changes tasks again, shaking his head. "My brain doesn't work that way. I spent a lot of my life fighting it, trying to stay focused and do things the conventional way, but that just isn't me. It doesn't work for me."

Still, he hasn't answered my question. But I stay silent and watch as he sets up a phone, new from the box, installing a SIM card, and downloading apps and emails and inputting phone numbers and I don't know what else.

His stance is relaxed but alert, his thumbs move at a wild pace, switching between the device he's setting up and the one he tagged from the bedside table. His brows are lowered, tight with concentration.

I wait patiently, happiness surging through me each time he takes a second to glance up at me. And when he sets both phones down on the counter behind me and smiles at me, my worries practically melt away.

Well, mostly.

Because even though that smile is captivating and draws me in, Teague's hands are in constant motion. Moving the syringe, sliding the packets around, arranging them and rearranging them again, and before I know what's happening, I feel the cold swipe of an alcohol swab against the top of my ass.

"Wait, you didn—"

My protest is cut off when his mouth crushes mine, his tongue licking inside with a toe-curling kiss that steals my breath and scrambles my brain. He grabs my hips and tugs me toward him, and I almost miss the pinch of the needle sliding into my flesh.

My gasp turns into a moan as his teeth sink into my lower lip, that bite of pain enough to distract me from chip being imbedded beneath my skin.

"You're so brave. You did it. So fucking proud of you,

hummingbird. And now it's your turn." His words at uttered against my lips, his mouth still *right there*.

Distracting.

Deliberate.

Precise.

He continues to explore my mouth, kiss a path across my jaw and along my neck, only pulling away when he places a fresh syringe in my hand.

Teague straightens to his full height and turns where he's bracketed between my legs. He makes quick work of his belt and unbuttons his trousers, pushing them low on his left hip. The defined ridge of muscle that wraps around his side, bulges and flexes with the movement and the top curve of his ass is exposed.

He cleans the skin and guides my hand and the syringe into place.

"Ready?"

Wide-eyed, I nod though just barely.

Together, we push on the needle, piercing his skin. "Press on the plunger, Truie. Mark me as yours. Make it so we'll never lose one another again."

I lock eyes with him.

"You can do it." A muscle tics at the sharp corner of his jaw as I do what he's asking.

When it's done, he presses his lips to mine and kisses

me softly, gently. Almost reverently, as if the act of inserting micro-chips in each other's backsides is a covenant.

And again, while he distracts me with his talented mouth, he taps his phone to my tracker and the other phone against his. Each elicits a quick beep, one vibrating against my skin.

That done, Teague pulls back, searching my face for, I don't know, signs of distress maybe? But there are none.

No distress.

No fear.

No panic.

"There. We're linked. Do you want me to show you how the app works now, or...?"

I don't know what it is about being tied to Teague in such a creepy, stalker-ish way, but I push the phones from his hands and pull him in tight. Desire flares low in my belly as I breathe him in. His auburn waves are too long, curling by his ears and at the nape of his neck.

His scruff glistens in the soft light.

I want to touch him and be touched.

I want to erase the nightmares that sex evokes in my mind, and replace them with something good, something pure. Something that doesn't involve pain and bleeding and—God, there's no other way to describe it—hate.

I want Teague to make me feel *more*.

"N-not now." I frame his face with my hands and guide him back to my mouth. "That's not what I want at all."

Chapter 16

Magic

TEAGUE

Soft hands frame my face, my stubble a rough rasping contrast as Truie takes what she wants. Her kiss is confident but almost tentative. Her delicate fingers seek purchase as they slide toward the back of my head, twisting through the hair I'd meant to get trimmed. When she pulls at the pieces curling behind my ears, I'm fairly certain I'll never cut it in such a way that *this* is no longer an option.

The need to be careful with her is waging a fierce battle with the urge to fuck her and make her mine. It's a battle I'm well acquainted with.

My dick is used to the literal ups and downs of this

dance with Truie. We've been doing it for ages, but the frequency has ramped up since I grabbed her from the cemetery.

"You'll have to use your words, hummingbird. What is it that you want?" I tuck my chin, pulling my head back so I can properly search her eyes.

I've spent every night since pulling her into my orbit, watching her sleep, most of them with her curled up in a tight ball until she's passed out. And when that happens, she loses all restraint, burrowing into my heat, draping herself across my chest.

But always on her terms.

Always at her speed.

Always her choice.

I grip her hips firmly, holding her in place as I angle my hips away. I want this woman. I want her badly. I just don't want to scare her by waving around the evidence of just how much.

"You." It's the only thing she gives me for an answer. Her voice is nervous, barely above a whisper. Where she was so strong setting out her terms for me to insert the tracker, now her touch is tentative, almost clumsy and unsure.

Jesus, the way I want her to feel powerful again, like she was moments ago. Like she was before.

Fucking before. The comparison, the then and now, the fact that there is a before and that the after is just so different.

"More, hummingbird. You need to give me more."

"That-that's what I want. More. I-I-I..."

The tips of her fingers trace the shape of my jaw, my neck, and skitter along my collarbones, dipping into the hollows and mapping each ridge.

Her touch is electrifying. Every one of my nerves endings is on fire and ready to explode. Hell, if she touches me anywhere south of my belt, I'm pretty sure I'll be done for. The last thing I want to do is to come in my pants like a fucking teenager.

I lose her touch as her hands twist together in her lap, shaking. Trembling like she's scared. That's a hard no for me.

"Truie, love"—I slide my hands from her hips to wrap around hers to calm the tremors—"there is not a rush. No hurry. We don't have to be on any kind of a timeline for this. I'm not going anywhere, yeah? And if I did, you could find me in a heartbeat now. Maybe we should take a minute, look at how the tracker works and—"

Blonde curls bounce wildly as she shakes her head. Brows pulled together and eyes wide, Truie insists, "No, not now. I... I just want... I want to be normal, but I'm... I don't think I know what to do, which is so... God, it just doesn't make sense."

"Oh, my sweet, sweet little hummingbird. Of course you're not normal, you're so much more. So perfectly special. You deserve to be worshipped, to be taken care of, loved. When the time is right, fear won't enter into it at all." I know I should be stressing that with the right person she won't be afraid. But I'd be lying if I said I'd be okay with her seeking out someone else to take care of any of her needs. It would fucking kill me.

A tear glistens in Truie's eye, and she blinks a handful of times trying to will it away. "This is so dumb." She pulls further into herself, twisting out of my hold and hopping off the counter. She steps away, putting space between us that I sure as hell don't want.

"What are you doing?"

"It-it's okay. Y-you don't have to, um... I think maybe it's too hard, asking too much from you." Sadness and frustration lace each and every word, shooting daggers straight through my heart.

The fucking tap dance, going round and round and never catching our own tails, is completely out of control.

I tag her hand and hold on. "Truie. Love. Hummingbird. There is no one in the world I want to be with aside from you." I crouch down so we are eye to eye. There is no room for misunderstanding here. "I assure you. I want nothing more than to take you to bed. I want to fuck you. Don't doubt that for a second. But I made a promise not to hurt you and I won't. I'll not lay a hand on you until you're ready, no matter how blue my balls become. You, love, you are in control. Whatever we do, it's at your pace. You want me to kiss your pussy again, I'll do it. Fucking happy to taste you, watch your cheeks turn pink, and see that sweet, satisfied smile on your face."

She shakes her head a-fucking-gain. The desire to slay her monsters, real and those in her nightmares, rears up in me.

"Come on. Come to bed and"—her gaze whips to mine—"you make the rules." I move past her, her hand still held firmly in mine and guide her back to my—*our*—bedroom. Because I'll be damned if anyone other than her will ever see the inside of that sacred space.

She follows me, and I loosen my grasp, giving her the option to sever our connection. Thank fuck, she does no such thing.

I stand at the side of the bed and with slow, deliberate movements, work the fastenings of my trousers free and let them drop to the floor.

Her gaze drops immediately, taking in the straining fabric of my boxer briefs.

"Shit, Tig, I d-don't know if I can..." Truie casts her eyes down.

The nickname, as often as I heard it growing up, has me stopping in my tracks as it spills from her lips. "You remember that?"

"What?"

"Haven't been called that by anyone since the night I pulled you out. You remember that?"

She sits on the edge of the mattress, searching her memories. "Yes?"

Nervous to thoughtful to pensive, and now frustration and self-flagellation are fighting for the limelight.

"Fuck, I'm b-broken. Why d-do you even want to b-bother with me?" The sudden reversion back to stuttering kills me, but those words pierce my heart.

"Look at me, Truie." I kneel down in front of her and tilt her beautiful face to meet my gaze. "You are the strongest woman I have ever met. You're not broken. Maybe a little bent, but you are not broken. Do you understand me?" At her subtle nod, I continue, "Now, I'm going to crawl into bed and lay down, flat on my back. What you do with that is up to you. I'm yours. Yours to touch. Yours to explore. Yours to play with, anything you want. If you want to curl up next to me and sleep, then that's what we'll do, yeah?"

Her teeth sink into her bottom lip making the prettiest little indents and, no matter how tight my control, my dick flexes. Christ, I want her bad.

"Sorry. It's biology, but I swear to you, I'll not move a single muscle unless you tell me to." I rock back on my toes and push to standing.

The cold sheets rustle as I sit down and slide between them, all of the warmth from earlier leached away, and my skin pulls tight into goose flesh.

Truie turns, her knee hiked up, body twisted as she looks her fill.

I fold my arms, tucking my hands behind my head, and try to relax. "I'll stay just like this."

"Until I tell you otherwise," she says.

"Until you tell me otherwise," I confirm.

Her gaze sweeps up my body, and I can feel each spot it touches like the sweetest teasing caress.

My blood pumps slow and heavy through my veins, much of it opting to go south. I grit my teeth and mentally go through the steps of stripping my weapon and cleaning it to will my dick from going full mast, but there's no hiding when it thickens, pressing against the soft fabric of my briefs.

The mattress dips as she crawls up from the foot of the bed and perches next to me on her knees. "That's, uh..."

"All yours, hummingbird. You do that just by looking at me. Just by being you."

She reaches out and then pauses, her hand hovering just above my thigh. Timid. Unsure. "I can touch you? Like this?" Her eyes dart to mine then back to my dick—growing with every heartbeat—as she trails her fingers up the line of muscle from my knee.

"Anything you want," is what I tell her, while every fiber of my being begs for more, more, more.

A touch so soft it should be lethal, glides along the outline of my dick, tracing the length before following the ridge of my crown and pressing against the blunt head. I could die from the delicate touch.

"It looks uncomfortable." She wraps her hand around my shaft, shifting it in the confines of my briefs until it lays straight against my body, angled toward my hip. On a soft breath, she whispers, "Oh."

Indeed.

"That definitely feels better." A groan rumbles low in my chest as she continues to stroke and explore my cock. And with the next stroke, a dot of pre-cum wets the cotton. Never in my life have I hated anything as much as I hate my briefs in this god damn moment. I want to strip them off and roll her over. I want to worship her the way she's meant to be.

My biceps bulge, and my hands tremble against the back of my head with the effort of restraint.

Truie slides her fingertips beneath the waistband and skims along the sensitive skin of my lower abs. When she lifts the wide elastic, my cock surges, laying fully erect against my belly.

I have to shove my head into my clasped hands to stop myself from reaching out. I ache to touch her, and the craving to taste her is almost overwhelming. I swallow hard, my mouth watering at the mere thought. I'm coiled tight like a spring ready to bounce.

"Lift."

I open my eyes, staring deep into hers. "Are you sure?"

At her nod, I arch my back and lift my hips off the mattress. Truie tugs at the tight fabric, sliding it down my legs until I can't help but kick them off. And then, *then* she has me totally naked and completely at her mercy.

Her wicked fingers and innocent touch trail fiery paths along my skin. She reaches between my legs and cups my balls, gently rolling the tight, swollen sac in her palm.

I have to count the letters of the alphabet, recall the number of lives I've taken, recite the blessed rosary, in order not to blow. She is literally killing me, and I can only think of one way I'd prefer to go. But that's her choice. I gave her control, complete control, over every step of this, so if I die with my balls cradled in her soft hand, then I'll be fucking grateful for the gift that is.

Her touch moves to my shaft, tracing the vein on the underside, teasing, touching. Pre-cum beads, and she rubs it delicately, playing with me, taking her time exploring me. Torturing me. And then Truie, my dear sweet little hummingbird, parts her lips and sucks on her finger.

Nope. This is what's going to kill me. This is how I'll fucking die.

Her eyes widen, and a smile pulls at her lush lips as she hums.

Fuck my life, this is *not* how I want to go out. No, I have to live long enough to see her mouth stretched wide as she swallows my cock. I cannot die until I've experienced that.

Either God's been listening to my prayers, or the rosary wasn't as bad a recitation as guilt had me thinking, because Truie does exactly that. She curls over me, hand grasping my dick, and slides her sweet lips around me.

Tremors wrack my body and it takes everything I have not to thrust into her mouth. To keep my hands where they are and not weave my fingers through her hair, to not hold her still and fuck her hot, wet, perfect mouth.

"*Fuck*. God, fucking hell," I groan through gritted teeth. My balls pull tight, dangerously tight. I'm going to traumatize this woman and embarrass myself in the process. "Careful, hummingbird. I'm trying to hold back, but your mouth is fucking perfect. God, please, baby, please..."

She is, in fact, decidedly *not* careful.

"Darlin', I'm going to—"

She hollows her cheeks, drawing the life right out of me. Through my fucking dick.

I see stars.

I transcend planes of existence.

I see the personification of Heaven staring up at me, bracketed by my thighs, lips stretched wide around my cock, her eyes dancing with delight.

For the briefest of moments, I forget myself, forget the vow I made to not move, and I haul her up until she's splayed across my body. I kiss her. Plunder her mouth, licking inside, and I taste myself mixed with her. Best fucking thing ever.

I lose myself in kissing her as my breathing comes back to something resembling normal. My hands skim the slight, round curve of her ass. I give each of the perky globes a squeeze and press her to me.

My dick rubs against her clit, and I get the most perfect little moan that I greedily swallow down.

It takes way too long for my brain to come back online.

"Christ, I'm sorry. I made you a promise and broke it immediately."

Her eyes are blown wide, her lips swollen and abused, and the smile pulling at the corners of her mouth is nothing short of magic.

"S'okay. I, um, I liked it. That. I liked doing that."

I pull her lower lip free from where she has it trapped between her teeth. She's going to resurrect my body and be the death of me all over again saying shit like that. "You liked swallowing my cock?"

"I liked... I liked the power? Like that you... You know."

A question. A question and she can't finish that sentence. "Power is in your words, hummingbird. If you like something, you need to own it. Say it like you mean it. And say the word, yeah. You like that I what? Tell me?"

"That you...finished?"

I hoist a brow high and push at the curls tumbling around her face. "Try again."

She takes a breath and then another, gathering herself for the task I've set before her. Jesus, it's hard on both of us, because her discomfort has her squirming. On top of me. Her pussy rubbing against my dick.

She rocks her hips, gliding over me from root to tip, using me to make her feel good. She hauls her knees up until she's got better leverage, the literal upper hand, and gasps, "I liked making you lose control. I liked that I did that."

"Mm. Made you feel brave, powerful, yeah?"

She dips her chin as she slides along my length.

"And now? Does this make you feel powerful?" I plant my hands on her hips, not moving her. Not even guiding her, but the need to touch her is overwhelming.

Her back arches, thrusting her tits out and exposing the delicate line of her neck as she works herself up.

"You look so beautiful making yourself feel good. Pink is such a good color on your cheeks." When she's ready, I'm going to love seeing that pink on her ass.

Every slide of her pussy, every brush of her clit, has her panting and gasping and moaning. Her arousal coating me until my dick is shiny with it and hard as stone.

"You're close, hummingbird, but not close enough, are you? What do you need? How can I help you get what you want?"

"More? I need more." She grinds against me hard, and then slides up farther, pausing when my blunt head notches against her opening. She pauses, her eyes dart to mine, questioning, asking permission? Waiting to see if I'm going to go back on my vow and yank her control away. Slam into her and take and take and take.

I won't do that. I already failed her by laying hands on her when I told her I wouldn't, I refuse to take this choice from her no matter how badly I want to be inside her.

Chapter 17

Constellation

TRUIE

He is right fucking there.

My body is humming, pulled taut and ready to come apart. I rock back and allow Teague to slip just inside. Just a little and not nearly enough.

"Your rules," he rumbles. "You're in control. Take what you want and only what you want. You're all that matters here, hummingbird." His voice sounds like honey dipped in gravel, strained and rough, but so, so sweet.

I rock back and forth, barely taking him inside me. An inch, maybe two.

He said I was brave, that I'm not broken, only bent. I want to believe him. I want to think I'm powerful, that

I'm in control. That I can ask for what I need, take what I want, and allow myself to feel without the darkness threatening to drag me under.

I stop. Stop moving. Doubting. Wondering. Wishing.

I hover above him, hands on the hard rounded muscles of his pecs, his cock just barely inside me, and stare into his warm brown eyes.

His chest rises and falls like he's running a race, his lids are low, but he never breaks eye contact. "You have all the control This is all about you... what you want... what you need. All you have to do is take."

The last word is barely out of his mouth when I allow myself to drop, to slide down his long, thick cock until my ass meets his hips. The air rushes out of me in a satisfied sigh. There's not enough room in my body for his dick and my lungs. It's okay. Perfectly okay, because I don't need air anymore. I don't need anything because this is it. The end of me. The end of him. The beginning of *us*.

I rock my hips, sliding up and down, desperate for the friction and scared as hell. My head tips back, and my eyes fall closed. The pressure that's been building in me, filling me and making me feel empty all at the same time explodes. My mouth opens on a silent scream, and the world around me expands until I can't take it anymore.

When Teague's words filter in through the haze of my orgasm, they're almost reverent. "There it is That's my good girl. Look at how well you take me, fucking gorgeous, hummingbird. Christ you're magnificent. I've never seen anything so beautiful in my entire life." My arms shake and threaten to give out. "Come here," he murmurs, hands sliding from my hips up my back until my head is cradled in one of his strong hands.

I collapse onto him, my chest pressed against his as his free hand glides up and down my back, my arm, and smooths the hair away from my face.

Somewhere along the way, Teague has become my safe space. I'm not exactly sure when. I don't know what made it happen, but it did. And I have never felt as safe, truly safe, as I do in this moment.

I blink against the bright light streaming through the window and take stock of myself, the room—I'm alone. My muscles are sore, but there's no actual pain. I don't think I've ever had sex that didn't involve pain. And I had an orgasm. An amazing, earth-shattering, mind-blowing orgasm. That's never happened during sex for me either.

I slide out from between the sheets and walk silently to the en suite to pee. When I wash my hands, taking time to look at myself in the mirror. There are no bruises reflected back at me. No dried blood caked around freshly sliced skin. There's...there's no dried, crusty cum anywhere on my body. Again, I've never experienced that before.

What do I do with myself now? I'm utterly out of my depth and wild thoughts swirl through my head. Should I stay in the bedroom? Maybe I shouldn't have gotten out of bed without permission. Old panic pushes in at the corners, and my head threatens to go hazy with fear.

I tiptoe out of the bathroom and freeze, naked and completely exposed, at the sight of Teague leaning against the doorframe. "I'm sorry," I whisper, dropping my gaze to the floor.

He pads across the room, stopping right in front of me. He hooks a finger under my chin and lifts until my gaze meet his. "You have nothing to apologize to me for." His brows are low and pinched together, but his warm chocolate eyes are completely sincere. Concerned... for me?

"I'm the one who's sorry. I ran downstairs to start the

coffee pot when I should've stayed. Should have been here when you woke up." Strong arms wrap around me, pulling me flush against his warmth. "God, I'm so sorry. I fucked this all to hell."

Unease skitters through me at sudden contact, and I freeze.

His hold loosens, just a little bit. "Shit, tell me how to make this right?"

I shake my head, too stunned to speak. And let's face it, I'm not great with words on a good day, and right now, I'm teetering on the edge.

Teague presses his lips to the top of my head, and laughs. Which throws me.

"Hummingbird, you have queen energy burrowed deep down inside you. You showed it last night, so there's no denying it exists. I will spend the rest of my life proving to you that you are worthy."

The iciness I've carried with me to numb my pain begins to melt.

"Bath? Breakfast? Or do you want to go back to bed?"

I shiver because as warm as Teague is, the air in the cabin is cold. "A shower? Please? And then..." I shrug.

He guides me into the bathroom and flips on the taps in the huge stone and glass shower. Steam swirls almost immediately as Teague guides me under the spray dropping his low-slung lounge pants as he steps in behind me.

He pampers me, running his fingers through my hair, lathering and rinsing it. Concentrates on applying conditioner, working it through every strand and then rinsing that too. He washes me, from head to toe, gentle and full of care.

The contrast is stark between the time and care he took in making sure I was clean and the hurried pace with which he cleans himself. He twists the taps off and wraps me in a warm towel, using another one to pat the water from my limbs and squeeze it from my hair. When he's done, he wraps it around his waist and settles me in front of the mirror.

Each mundane task is completed with diligence. My hair is combed until it's snarl free and smooth. He holds up a finger indicating he'll be right back, reappearing with a fresh pair of lounge pants, a soft gray t-shirt, and a hoodie that is far too big for me. All of the clothes are, but I've been stealing them to wear this whole time. Being surrounded by him calms me. It keeps the anxiety from taking over and crushing me.

I pull on the items, one by one, drowning in their security.

When he's similarly dressed, Teague holds his hand out for me to take and leads me down to the main level.

"I got the fire started. Curl up there, and I'll bring you a coffee. Then we'll go over the tracking app and tech shit. As much as I want to hide away here with you, I'm going to have to go back to the estate and I can't do that unless I know you can find me."

I don't like the fact that he's going to leave me here alone, but even that takes a back seat to the fact that he wants me to be able to track his whereabouts. More iciness melts away.

Teague brings me coffee, perfectly doctored with cream and honey, and settles in next to me on the deep green sofa. He pulls a sleek phone from his pocket and grabs my hand, pressing my finger to the screen.

"The tracking screen is here. It updates in real time, allowing you to see exactly where I am." His eyes find mine, creasing at the corners as he smiles. "I dropped some numbers in your contacts. Winnie, Garrick. Me. And I attached the reading and shopping apps to my account. Order whatever you want. Deliveries will go to the estate—for safety reasons—but Garrick will bring anything you order. Sound good?"

I nod.

"Good. Now let me get you something to eat and then we can spend the day any way you want." He hands the phone to me, gives my thigh a quick squeeze, and stands. He leans down and takes my mouth, kissing me stupid and leaving me breathless.

While he cooks, I sit and stare at the flames, their dance choreographed to music I wish I could hear, accented with crackles and pops. I'd be happy as a pig in shit if I never had to leave this place.

Teague brings me a plate filled with fresh fruit and eggs and toast and...

"Is this b-bacon?" I hold my breath, afraid of the answer.

He plops down beside me, bouncing on the sofa cushion. "Turkey bacon, hummingbird. I wouldn't dream of making real bacon."

The smell alone would have sent me running from the house—unless the memories it evoked had me frozen in full-blown panic attack—if it were the real stuff. It clung to the clothes of the men who hurt me. The quantity they consumed surely should have killed them, but instead, it seemed to fuel them.

"Thank you." I pick at my food, taking small bites when Teague stares at me for too long, but truth be told, the fresh, sweet red berries are all I really want. The gesture is kind and so thoughtful, but anxiety is my constant companion, and food is almost always a crap shoot.

Teague cleans his plate in the time it takes me to

finish my berries, so I hand him the rest of mine. He leans forward to set the empty plates on the coffee table and the pale gray t-shirt shifts, stretching as his muscles flex.

Without thinking, I reach out and trace the bumps and divots that make up the landscape of his back. Thick muscle frames his spine and expands out, wrapping his ribs and shoulders in strength.

Cinnamon-colored freckles create a constellation that disappears beneath the hem of his shirt.

He lets me trace a path from one to the next and the next and the one after that, his skin pebbling in tight goosebumps. I scrape my nail down his back, reversing the path, and a low groan rumbles from his lungs.

"Christ, don't stop. Feels so good."

I pause at the waistband of his lounge pants, then follow it around as he leans back, fully slouched into the plush cushions. His lids are heavy, his eyes dark with desire.

A warm palm lands on my knee and stays there. He makes no move other than the gentle pressure as he fully gives in to whatever this is.

He lets me explore, touch, and discover more of the ticklish spots that have him squirming out of my touch and the sensual ones that have him trying to get closer.

And all of that happens with no complaints. He simply watches me.

"Hummingbird, I love letting you have free reign of my body, feeling your touch getting more confident, but you keep teasing me like this, I'm gonna be tempted to put you on your back and fuck you good." There's no venom, just heat and a delicious promise. "You think you're ready for that?"

Am I? I have no idea. Trauma is a fickle bitch, but I am so damned tired of being a slave to her. If I don't test my limits, I'll never know if I'm free from the cage, and there is no one else I'm more comfortable with than Teague.

So, I drag the tip of my finger along the deep groove of muscle that wraps around his hip pointing to his groin, my touch feather light. I trail along his inner thigh, almost touching him, but not quite.

I'm in control. I'm in control. I'm...

In a blink of an eye, I'm on my back, bracketed by Teague's arms as he hovers over me. I'm okay. I didn't panic. I haven't shut down. No dark thoughts push their way in, and there isn't a single tremor that's based in fear. My body heats, desire pooling low in my belly.

"You good?"

I dip my chin keeping my eyes locked on his.

"If that changes, you tell me. I want your words, though. Can you do that?"

"Yes" barely tumbles from my lips, and he's on me. Devouring my mouth, licking a path down my body, clothes piling up on the ground around us.

He settles between my legs, his shoulders too broad for the tight space on the couch. He pushes at the back of my thigh, lifting my leg until it's propped on the back of the couch, giving himself more space to maneuver.

He licks my pussy and sucks my clit into his mouth, humming. He worships my body.

I feel one finger enter me, then two. He curls his fingers, rubbing gently at a spot inside me that I thought was nothing more than a myth. When he sucks hard on my clit, I tremble through the explosion of my orgasm. Each one is somehow better than the last. I want to live in this moment forever.

Gentle kisses wind in a trail up my body as Teague crawls over me. When he reaches my mouth, he asks, "You ready?"

It takes a handful of breaths for me to find my words. "Yes?"

"That a question?"

I shake my head and he grunts out, "Good," as his hips snap forward. He fills me with a single thrust, bottoming out. He drops his forehead to mine and mumbles, "*Fuck.*"

I cling to Teague's shoulders, twine my fingers through his auburn waves and fist them tight as he moves his body in wild and only faintly controlled chaos. He moves like a man consumed, hitting a spot deep inside me that makes me see stars. I come again, and again, and when his skin is sweat slicked and damp curls cling to his forehead, he presses his thumb to my clit. I shake my head. I don't think I can do it. I don't think I have it in me to come again.

"You want me to stop?" He pants, hips still, but planted deep.

I shake my head again.

"Need your words, hummingbird."

My body rolls, seeking pleasure I'm not sure I understand, because this can't be normal. It can't be. This many orgasms need a safety warning.

"No," I say on a moan as I twist and rotate my hips chasing a high I don't just want, but need, as much as my next breath. "Please don't stop."

Chapter 18

Retribution

TEAGUE

The last thing I wanted to do this morning was drag my sorry ass out of bed to go meet with my boss.

Does Christophe need me to do my job, look into why some very sketchy shit is going on in our world, chase down the asshole who's going batshit, flipping rocks for that fucking file full of transgressions? Yeah. If I'm honest, he really does.

But I was wrapped around Truie, her tit in my right hand, my left firmly tucked between her sweet thighs. So, my shitty attitude really needs to be overlooked. Sacrifices have been made on my part, and I deserve a fucking medal.

"Tell me what you know," Christophe demands through my speakers because this couldn't even wait for me to get to the house.

It takes serious restraint not to roll my eyes like a petulant child because nine times out of ten, he knows exactly what I know, and this is a nine, for sure.

"Desmond is a pain in my ass and stirring shit every chance he gets. Been blowing up my phone for the past week. For the last two days, I blocked him." That asshole isn't worth my time.

"You had better things to do. Take care of," he amends. "You give the girl Winnie's number?"

"And Garrick's. Hate that she's not coming in with me." He knows, he's heard that more than enough, and let's be honest, Christophe wouldn't be caught dead with his woman beyond his immediate reach.

Not now. Not since he's finally gotten her.

But I'm not the big boss, here. I don't make the rules, I just have to tap dance around them, bend them when necessary, and find a way to function without raising too many red flags.

"She's safer hidden away there," he says, simply. As if this—any of this—is a minor thing.

If the tables were turned, he would not willingly leave Winnie tucked away somewhere and go about his business. Even back when he couldn't be with her, he had me keeping eyes on her. Following her every move, ensuring her safety.

Falling for the girl who always had her back was never part of the assignment. But here we are, dumb and fucking obsessed.

"You need to go see him. Sit down with Desmond, maybe some of your other family members and see what they know. Do it separately. I don't want to give Des any reason to... blah blah blah. You fucking know what you need to do. We've got to find what they're looking for and get him and the others off our backs."

Don't I fucking know it.

"My family? You think any of them are going to tell me anything useful?" I glance in my rearview mirror. Red and blue lights flash behind me followed by a lovely *whoop* that just makes my damn day. "Fuck. Talk to you later." I disconnect the call and pull over to the side of the road. I ease to a stop, shift the gear into park, and set both hands on the top of the steering wheel.

Looks like I'm talking to Desmond sooner rather than later.

He raps on the window and rests his arm on the roof of my Range Rover, the other falling to his sidearm. Fucker thinks he's suave as shit.

I lower the window.

"Need you to step out of the car."

"Des. How are you this morning?"

"Step out of the car, Tig." His aviators are dark, almost completely hiding his eyes from me. Almost. But his brow shifts the smallest amount when he flicks his gaze over the roof of my car.

I don't get the chance to see what has his attention before the passenger door flies open and a telltale sting, followed by a fiery burn, flares in my neck. Whatever they shoot me up with works fast and my motor control withers away leaving me frustratingly aware and absolutely unable to do shit.

"Cousin. I've been looking for you. Been wanting to talk to you, catch up with you and the pretty little thing you're hiding away somewhere." Desmond leans on the door, hand hanging loose just to my left. They're right fucking there and I can't do a single thing. "Jesus, I can practically smell her on you. She's got a sweet pussy, doesn't she? Might have to get me another taste when I find her again."

Rage courses through me. The idea that he's touched Truie, tasted her, breathed the same fucking air as her, has my heart racing and my blood heating up in my veins. I want to break his fingers so he can never touch her again. Rip his tongue from his fucking mouth and set fire to it. Peel his skin from his body. Kill him slowly, painfully.

The passenger seat is filled with a body, and a mystery hand swipes my phone from the center console. It unlocks when my thumb is pressed to the screen and then disappears from my line of sight.

Silent seconds pass. Even though it looks it in every way, this is no simple traffic stop... not that anyone will notice. There are no other cars on this stretch of rural road. No one to mark the flashing lights or my Range Rover.

"Password's disabled, boss. You ready?"

My phone flies past my face and Desmond tags it out of the air, pocketing it. "Make sure the zip ties are secure when you get him moved. Fucking ginger genes. Who knows how long that drug will last in his system. I don't need it burning off while I'm driving."

I take small pleasure in the fact that Desmond and the asshole he employs work up a good sweat getting me moved from my vehicle to the rear cargo area of the police issue SUV.

"Jesus fuck, you've put on the pounds, haven't you?"

Of course I have. The last time Desmond and I got into it, we were kids, doing daily inventory on pubes and pit hair. He was bigger than me then, but now it's no contest. Or it wouldn't be if I could fucking move. Being this helpless, this vulnerable, is something I'm not at all familiar with. Because even back when we were kids and

Desmond had the size advantage, I still kicked his ass on the regular.

The rough carpet burns as my face scrapes across it. Plastic bites into my skin as the zip ties are secured around my wrists and my ankles. I may not be able to move a fucking muscle, but I can feel every goddamn thing. I catalog it all, file every transgression away for later. When the time comes, I'll immerse myself in the cauldron of retribution and dole out an eye for an eye, pain for pain, scar for fucking scar. And then I will put this cunt down like a rabid dog.

"Give him another hit. Just to be sure he stays down," Desmond orders.

Doors slam, closing me in, and when we start rolling, and the world dissolves into mist.

I come to with the feel of concrete grinding against my knees and a chain around my neck. My hands are still bound tightly behind my back—nothing's changed there. Everything hurts but still, something seems off.

Shit, everything feels off.

When the leather strap slides from beneath my

arms, tugging at where it catches across my chest, I feel its support give way. The slack is taken up by the chain, and my chin snaps. My body goes completely rigid to keep from hanging myself and the shift grinds the concrete further into my knees.

I hang and try to reposition myself, making subtle adjustments until the pain and threat of asphyxiation find an unlikely balance. "*Fuck.*"

"Mm. You're certainly that. How're you feelin', cousin?"

The accent Desmond keeps under wraps is enjoying a rare freedom. The lilt would be comforting if it were coming from almost any other family member.

But this one? This one I want to annihilate.

"Fuck you."

He strolls around me, leisurely, stopping just off to the side.

He's not as dumb as I wish he was. If he'd stopped right in front of me, I could have lurched forward and taken a good shot to his groin.

"You're mad, then?" he asks, folding his arms over his chest. "Is it that I've bested ye? Or that I had the girl first? Fuckin' killin' ye that I tasted her, that I fucked her. That I left my mark on her and you got the scraps, yeah? She probably came panting after ye, hoping you could give her ride like she had wit' me. Ah, but I ruined her for ye. She had a nice tight cunt, could barely get my cock in her all the way. Poor girl probably couldn't even tell if you were in or not."

I know better. I do. But all I see is red.

A growl surges from my belly as I lunge for him, teeth bared and ready to tear at whatever I can latch on to. I'll tear him apart one bite at a time if I have to.

Desmond jumps back a step, having miscalculated just how sharply his words would land. When he's soundly out of range, he laughs. Higher than normal, definitely some panic laced throughout, but the fucker laughs at me.

"Settle. You're like a leashed cat, losing your senses and flailing against your tether. You give me what I need, I'll let you go. You can have what's left of her." He bends at the waist, staring me straight in the eyes. "If there's anything left to claim, that is."

The bend, that shit failure of spatial awareness, brings him just close enough for a quick jerk of my neck. Blood sprays across my clothes and down his shirt after a satisfying crunch, and his nose sits slightly left of center.

It takes a moment to get my breath back when the pressure from the chain loosens. I'd do it again and again and again, if it were my only retaliation. I'd choke myself on it if I knew nothing would come back on Truie. But that's not a luxury I can afford with this particular adventure.

"What do you want?" My voice is rough, sounding like I've swallowed a fist full of glass and washed it down with acid. "How long have I been here?"

Where isn't even a question. I'd recognize the storage room of my uncle's shop anywhere. The parts shelves line the cinderblock walls. A drain sits in the floor. The smell of used oil and gasoline permeates the space. We've all spent time in this room, though usually not cuffed and dangling from the ceiling.

"The file. I need the fucking file, Tig. I know you've got it. Know she took it with her when you carried her out of Alain's basement—"

"What file? That's what you're on about?"

Desmond catches himself as he bends, trying to get into my space once again, and straightens to look down on me. He exaggerates his enunciation, "The fuckin' file. I don't know how she got it, or what ye've done with it, but I fuckin' need it, right fuckin' now." He's red-faced and nearly screaming by the time he finishes his demand.

"I. Don't. Have. It," I shout right back. My snark is not appreciated.

There's a faint whistle in the air behind me before pain explodes through my hands. The strike was hard enough to break the zip ties, but what should be a relief is nothing but an explosion of pain.

"Where th' fuck is it?"

His question barely filters through my scream. My vision goes hazy when I try to lift my mangled hands to inspect the damage. A tire iron lands in the center of my chest, sliding up under my chin until I have no choice but to meet Desmond's gaze.

"Why?" I cut the question short when the curved socket end raps sharply against my chin, my teeth taking the brunt of the force. I spit out a bloody white shard, hitting Desmond's boot with a chunk of my tooth and a good dose of DNA.

"Because with Alain out of th' picture, whoever holds th' file, holds th' power. He thought that L'Ourson bitch had it, that th' little swine gave it up to her. That was half th' reason Alain stole Henri's daughter."

"Other half was because he was depraved," I spit out.

"Taught me everything I know, cousin. Gave me and the boys free rein down in his basement. We could do anything we wanted down there. Hit the bitches, hurt them, fuck them, carve them up, kill them…anything. Those cunts were at our mercy." His teeth are bared, lips pulled back in a snarl.

It takes everything I have to focus. "And why would

this file be down there in the house of horrors, huh? Which one of you miscreants took it with you to go have a little fun? Who's the fucking eejit who lost track of it while sticking his dick in a hole?"

The way his face flames red is a good indicator that the eejit is, in fact, my lovely cousin—the newly minted police detective and a wee cunt. Sadly, I don't see the fistful of brake lines come at me from the side. I do feel the slice. I feel my skin pull apart and the warmth of my blood as it seeps from the four gapping wounds across my cheek.

Chapter 19

Comfort

TRUIE

The first couple of hours were nice. I sat by the fire, coffee in hand and watched the flames dance to silent music. I thought about all the ways my body was sore and the very tall, very strong, very delicious reason they were that way. I thought about the landscape of ridges and valleys mapped by his freckles and all the ways I wanted to explore and taste him.

That's a lie.

That's what I wanted to be doing and thinking. Instead, I sat by the fire and missed Teague.

I thought about how long he might be gone, and when he'd be back. About what he was doing, how he was keeping me safe.

And what all of that meant.

I thought about the SIM card. I'd never looked at what was on there. I hadn't dared, but I knew it was important. Figured it was a lot of damning information. Why else would the man have been bragging to his friend that he had it? That he'd swiped it right out from under the *Parrain's* nose. That he could rule the world with it? All while he dragged a knife through my skin.

Teague hadn't balked at the sight of the crisscrossed lines; he'd traced them the way I traced designs in his freckles. He kissed my scars with such tenderness and care.

"Look at you, little hummingbird," he'd said. "Look at the way your body tells the story of everything you've lived through. Every mark your skin bears is another moment you survived. I would lay down my life for the chance to worship every single one of your marks."

I'd squirmed as he trailed his finger over the lattice work of scars. I hate them. I hate all of them. Most of the time, I keep them covered, hide them away. I don't even look at them anymore. I haven't since they'd healed when I was in the hospital.

"Each and every one of them is a reminder of *them*. The things they did to me, the things they took." Tears rolled down my cheeks as the recounting tumbled from my lips. In all the time I was in therapy, all the hours spent in that psychologist's chair, I never bared my soul the way I did with Teague last night. I inhaled and held that breath while I admitted, "I want to rip them off, cut them out of my skin, burn them away. But those marks are on my soul too. I don't know how to do this. How to keep going with that constant reminder written all over me."

I tried to push him away, to cover the reminders of just how broken I was, but he was right there. His face hovering above the lines, his breath skating across my skin, touching me. Caressing me. Treating each mark with a reverence I just didn't fully understand.

His lips brushed against my skin as he said, "Let me show you. Let me paint your scars and show you just what a masterpiece you are." And then he traced those scars, those marks of Hell, with the tip of his tongue until I was squirming for an entirely different reason.

Sex was... God, how many of my fucked-up emotions were tied to that act. At seventeen, it was a resounding *fuck you* to the expectations of my father. *Be pure. Save yourself. I'll decide who the man worthy of your innocence is.* That was a hard no thank you from me.

I'd seen the way he wielded that power with my mother before she finally got free of him. If only she'd been allowed to take me when she left. She'd warned me not to give up control, not to yield power and let anyone else make decisions for me like that. It was with her encouragement that Winnie and I decided to steal out of town the minute we were done with high school. A pipe dream that became more of a pipe bomb is what happened.

But at least I'd taken control of my own future and fucked the first boy who'd shown interest. Took that little cherry and stomped all over it—me, not him. He was a sweet thing, fumbling and timid, and totally unsure of what to do. We both were, but it was a means to an end. And that end? Yeah, my father blew his lid. Told me I was ruined, tainted. Fucking worthless.

Who knows, maybe the very act I thought gave me power was the one that took it all away. My father had me kidnapped. My father had me thrown in that dark and terrifying place. I'll never know if he sanctioned the abuse, the torture, the hell I endured, but I do know that he didn't lift a finger to help me.

It would have been wrong to celebrate a person's death. I was already in a psych ward when it happened—I didn't need to give anyone a reason to keep me there indefinitely—but I did not waste a single tear on the man who thought so little of me. When the doctor told me my father'd been found dead in his office, a pot of bee balms just outside the window and a hummingbird sipping at the nectar next to it, I'd simply nodded. I was broken after all. The expected reaction from me was complete and total breakdown... or nothing at all.

I chose nothingness. I put up the walls I needed to protect me. I spent a ridiculous amount of time chasing the illusion of dreams. I didn't know it was Teague I was chasing—his voice, his touch, the gentle care he took in holding me safe against his chest. Those walls were keeping the shit reality away from my perceived dreams.

But it turns out, Teague is real. His heart, his touch, that melodic voice, soft and lilting, murmuring against my skin and wrapping me in safety. All very real.

And very much not here right now.

Missing him when I thought he was nothing more than the figment of my broken mind was hard. It hurt.

Missing him now is so much worse, even if it's only been a handful of hours.

I open the phone he left with me and tap into the location app. I can see his dot, blinking strong and sure, but I don't have a clue where he is. It's been so long since I was free to roam around town. And I have no idea where Christophe's estate is in comparison to the places I do know. Or whether that blinking orange light is there.

I open the messaging app and tap on Winnie's contact.

Me: Hey. It's Tru.

Minutes pass and no response comes. I switch back to the tracking app and watch that little light blink—slow and steady. Its persistence bolsters me, gives me hope, a connection that I didn't think possible.

The phone buzzes, startling me from this newfound calm that is only attributable to Teague.

> Winnie: TRU! holy shit, sweetie, are you ok?

Me: I am. How are you?

Even in text, my conversation is stilted. At least my fingers don't stutter.

> Winnie: good. so good. except…

Me: ?

> Winnie: nothing. i'm good. where are you?

Me: No. Finish that. Except what? You can tell me if you're not really okay. If you're scared, maybe Teague can bring you here. It's safe…but I don't know exactly where here is.

> Winnie: so… he's left? what time? do you think he'll get here soon?

I tilt the screen and reread her last message, unease roiling in my belly.

> Me: He left hours ago. He's not there?

Dots dance and tease, stopping then starting up again. Each cycle ramping up my fear. But what could happen to Teague? It's not like he's some frail young girl who assholes could get a jump on and throw in the trunk of their car, right?

> Me: Winn?

> Winnie: he's not here, not answering his phone. Christophe is pissed. i'm actually glad you're not here…tensions are high.

Always worried about me, so in tune with my feelings. Fear and panic have ruled the past couple of years, and Winnie has navigated that minefield every step of the way. I appreciate her concern, but maybe this is a good time for those feelings to bloom.

> Me: What do you mean he's not there?
> Where else would he be? His light is
> blinking so nothing is wrong, right?

> Winnie: his light?

> Me: His tracking light. It's blinking.
> That means…

What does it mean? I didn't ask if it would go out if the person, the host, were to die. I never thought I'd need to know a detail like that—why would I?

> Me: He showed me how to use a
> tracking app. So I'd always know
> where he was. So I wouldn't worry. But
> I'm worried, Winn. I'm scared.

> Winnie: What app?

Something about those two words, the sharpness of the demand feels different. Off. Like it's not my friend. My hands start to shake. However ridiculous the thought that I wouldn't stutter in text, I'm rethinking that. Because I have to delete a handful of extra letters before I hit Send.

> Me: Who is this?

> Winnie: Christophe. What app, Truie?
> Send me a screenshot of his location.

I bounce over to the tracking app and play with the buttons, unable to capture a screenshot, no matter what I do. With tears threatening, I pass that information on to Winnie—Christophe—and wait. And wait.

> Me: What's happening?
>
> Me: Winn?
>
> Me: Please. I know you want to shelter me and keep me safe, but don't lock me out. Not now. Not with this. Winnie, tell me what's happening?

I pace in front of the floor-to-ceiling windows, eyes darting from the phone's screen to the vast plane of unbroken snow and back again. A chill skates down my spine, wracking my body, and I turn back to the hearth. The embers are low.

Winnie's ignoring me. For the first time since forever, Winnie is deliberately shutting me out. Not the well-intentioned filtering or softening of information. Not the screening out of the really bad shit. She's taken away my choices, pulled them right out from underneath me, and has gone silent.

Gingerly, I set another log from the copper bin on top of the ash and orange glow, staring at the hint of life dancing amidst the darkness, willing it to life. I force myself to sit. To wait. To stare at the flames licking at the underside of the fresh piece of wood.

I don't know how long I wait, turning over how I feel, and how I've stranded myself by being a slave to my own trauma, just staring at the fire. But as that flame builds, as it takes root and grows stronger, I steel my spine. I sink into the choice of panic or power. I take the small bit of confidence I've found with Teague and let it smolder. Feed it and will it to grow.

When the fire inside me burns as hot and strong as the one in front of me, I pull myself upright and make my way to Teague's bedroom. I rifle through the bag he brought from the estate and find clothes he'd picked out for me. Clothes he bought and packed and brought here...for me.

I strip out of the oversized lounge pants and henley I stole from his closet and dress in the soft, carefully chosen items from the bag. Bralette and panties, leggings in soft pink and a big fuzzy sweater in the exact rosy mauve of the old cardigan that I always pulled close when I got scared at the L'Ourson's house.

How? How is this the exact color of my comfort sweater? How did he know?

Realization slams into me, nearly knocking the breath from my lungs. The attention, the concern, the way he's watched out for me since...since fucking when?

Teague has been patiently waiting in the shadows for me to what? Find myself? Find my strength? My sanity?

I found those things in him, with him.

Through him.

And now he needs me to be stronger than I've been in a really long fucking time.

I hit Garrick's contact bubble on my phone and count the rings.

On five, the line crackles and he answers. "Good afternoon, miss. How can I be of service?"

"Garrick, i-it's me, Tru. I know you're busy, but I need you to come get me. Teague said you know where I am."

"I do, Miss Cochonette, but Mr. Grey asked that I do everything in my power to keep you in place. He feels you're safest there. I'm sure you understand." His tone is kind while his words true to Teague's wishes.

But Garrick doesn't know what Teague feels in this moment, no one does. Tense matters, and what Teague felt before he left his house in the woods this morning is vastly different from what he's likely feeling right now. Going missing will do that. But he has me, and I know what it's like to be taken.

"I do understand—"

"Excellent. Then do tell, what is it you need? The estate is quite busy at the moment."

Every muscle in me constricts, cold sweat racing down my spine. I get that Garrick is stressed, just like everyone at that estate is. I'm sure Teague's uncharacteristic tardiness was a huge inconvenience, but his outright disappearance? That's enough to raise the stress levels to highs I'm not sure I can imagine. But I have my own set of standards for stress and worry and panic. And I'm fighting those with everything I have, because Teague needs me to.

"I know. I can imagine you're being pulled in several directions at the moment. But…but I can get us to Teague, Garrick. I can get us to him and"—I pause before spilling my darkest secret—"I know why they took him." Silence hangs heavy between us. "Please, Garrick. Please come get me."

Chapter 20

Ledger

TRUIE

Time, on paper, is an absolute. It doesn't bend, doesn't shift, it simply is. In crisis, it's slower than tectonic plates shifting.

That's how it feels waiting for Garrick to get to Teague's house. That's how it feels knowing that Teague is in trouble and I'm the one who holds the key to where he is.

Me.

Like God couldn't have picked a more incapable person to have that kind of power. Jesus, I'm a mess.

The pull to spiral and let my toxic shit take control is nearly impossible to fight. Being docile has been my comfort, my constant companion for so fucking long, it just feels safe.

Winnie was my grounding force through that time, but I still—*still*—haven't heard a peep from her. When I need her the most, she's disappeared.

That's something to deal with later, because if I let it eat me up, I won't have anything left to fight my internal battles and do what needs to be done with the external ones.

I have to talk to people I haven't had to before now, and I have to do it with efficiency. I must take control of myself, of my situation and the knowledge I have in my actual, literal hand and put it to use.

I have to find Teague, to get to him and save him. I have to saddle my weakness and be his strength. Christ, this is a mess.

A soft knock is my only warning before the lock clicks and the door opens inward. Garrick steps through, shutting the door behind him and I have to shove down the fear that hits when I'm shut into a room with a man. A man other than Teague... But this is more than just a damp, dank cinder block room, and Garrick has been nothing but kind, fatherly in all the ways mine never was.

"Miss Cochonette." He takes off his hat and nods to

me. "When you're ready... I'll bank the fire so we can depart." He hasn't moved from where he stopped just inside the front door—off to the side so he's not blocking the exit. Both hands are visible, gently cradling his hat and completely nonthreatening. His expression is soft, relaxed with an understandable edge of urgency.

He's waiting on me.

I'm in control.

I have the power to slow us down and cause Teague unfathomable harm, or to hand over the information I have and save the man I don't think I can live without.

"Yes. P-please. I'll g-go find a coat?" I step back, ready to take off for the bedroom and collect myself before having to put my safety in someone else's hands. To breathe before I have to speak. I did okay, only two little slips, but my stutter and elevated stress are never a good combination.

Garrick raises his left arm and steps forward. "I took the liberty of bringing one of Mr. Grey's coats for you, miss. It's my understanding that you prefer the warmth of the wool. Perhaps the heft of it offers a bit of security."

He extends the charcoal gray wool coat toward me but waits for me to approach him. Each action has my comfort in mind. I want to cry at the thoughtful way he deals with me.

"Thank you." I take the coat, and Garrick goes to the fireplace, efficiently banking the few remaining embers. I don't know if he notices the way I bury my face in the soft wool, the way I inhale the scent of Teague that clings to it, but he shows no indication that I'm weak or lacking in anyway.

When the house is closed down, I follow Garrick to the small, sporty roadster that seems wildly out of character for him.

"Mr. Grey and I felt that, should such a need arise, the large utility vehicle might cause you unnecessary stress." When I merely nod, he continues with a small smile, his eyes sparkling, "Plus, the roadster is a bit of an indulgence to drive. Shall we?"

He helps me into the low-slung car, jogging around the front to take his place behind the wheel. "If at any point, you're uncomfortable, please speak freely. I don't get the opportunity to drive her often and tend to let her run as she sees fit." His excitement for the fast car is evident.

"We're kind of in a hurry, so…"

The engine roars to life, hinting at the power beneath the hood.

"Time is indeed of the essence."

The trip to the estate passes in a blur, thrill and trepidation fighting for centerstage in my mind. Thrill edges forward, allowing me to prepare for the tornado that's about to hit.

Garrick ushers me through the door and into the dark, moody office off the entry way. The one I've spied Teague leaving with a scowl on his face. I may have even been in there, but the fuzzy haze that surrounds that thought is too much to process right now.

Christophe governs the space from behind the massive desk, tension rolling off of him in waves.

"Sit."

The harsh command makes me freeze, burrowing deeper into the wool coat I've yet to release.

"You're scaring her. Don't... You have to soften your tone."

My head whips around at the sound of Winnie's voice. She looks like shit. Red blotchy face, eyes swollen with tears, her hands shaking almost uncontrollably. It's like we've traded places.

"Winn—"

"Honeybee, you'll have your moment to grovel but right now, Tru and I have work to do." The harsh reprimand is in direct opposition to the way his eyes lick over her, caressing her. At any other time, it would be obscene, but something about the exchange and the way

Winnie abandoned our text conversation gives me pause.

"Please, Tru. Sit." Still all business, Christophe manages to soften it with the *please*, and I perch on the edge of the chair facing him. I pull my phone from where I've kept it in the inside pocket of the coat, close to my heart. My thumb hits the screen in the exact right spot, unlocking it to display the screen with the orange blinking light.

"Does... does the blinking stop if-if the person is no longer...if their heart does?" I can barely consider the fact that Teague might be gone, saying it out loud is entirely too much.

"I can't answer that without knowing the specs of the specific tracker." He plucks the proffered phone from my hand, and studies the screen before staring at me, hard. "How did he end up with the device? He told me it was for you, so he didn't lose you again."

"He had two. I, um, I protested being chipped like a dog—"

"That's not what it—"

"I understand that, but think about how that would be received, just for a second." Christophe's head snaps back when I interrupt, my voice soft but strong. "But Teague knew. He knew I would have a problem with handing over complete control and was prepared to match that energy and do the same. He had everything at his fingertips to give up the same control—to offer the same vulnerability—that he was asking of me." I glance over my shoulder at Winnie and turn back to the big, scary head of organized crime and give him all the attitude I can muster. "Now, are you going to help me find the man I love... help me find Teague?"

He huffs, lips tipping up on one side of his mouth, and pulls a sleek laptop toward him. The top is up and the screen shows a map of town with the tracking app overlaid on it. "I've got his location and men en route. But he wouldn't have been taken for no reason, so why don't you tell me what you have that this motherfucker thinks he's entitled to."

I push to standing, swaying a little at the sudden movement. "You know where he is? Why...why are we still here? Take me... I need—"

"You need to sit your ass down and talk." He raises a hand to stop my protest before it fully forms. "I know none of this is easy, but you have to know I have nothing but respect for you. You're safe here under my protection, but I need to know where the file is."

"W-what's in it that has everyone in this town losing their m-minds?"

"It's a list. An accounting ledger of who's done what... Fuck, of everything. Enough to ruin everyone...

who owes whom, who has dirt, and what they did. Not just body counts, but where the bodies are buried and the DNA that was left close by to frame someone when the time comes. Fucking everything."

"I-I didn't want to look, didn't want to know any of it because I've lived way too close to the edge of death and this kind of knowledge seems like a one-way ticket six feet under. So, I didn't. I just hid it. Kept it safe until…"

"Tru. Oh my God, you never told me. You never said anything about…"

"I couldn't." I turn so I can see Winnie as well as Christophe. Today isn't a day I want my back to anyone, no matter how close we are. Something in my gut tells me I'm not going to like the explanation behind Winnie's tears and puffy eyes. "There are a lot of reasons why, but that's a later thing." I turn back to Christophe. "For now, is that enough to get Teague back?"

He stands, buttoning the coat of his bespoke suit and straightening the cuffs. "There was never a minimum due for getting to Teague. Access to the app simply made things easier. The rest of this conversation can wait for now. I want to personally see to his immediate needs, and to deal with the assholes who took him. You're to stay here, understood? Under no circumstances do either of you leave the estate, and for the love of fucks"—his attention goes straight to Winnie—"don't talk to anyone besides each other. You have amends to make.

"Garrick, take the women to Miss Cochonette's suite and make sure they have whatever they need to be comfortable." Christophe stalks from the room, taking a mere fraction of the tension with him.

"What do you need to make amends for, Winn?" My shoulders are tight, back ramrod straight.

Winnie sinks deeper into the chair tucked in the corner of the office, shaking her head. "I'm so sorry."

"Ladies, if you please." Garrick sweeps a hand, inviting us to leave the dark office space behind.

We hold our silence close as we follow him through the hallways toward what was supposed to be my suite in this gilded prison. But I never spent the night in the beautifully appointed room. Instead, I clung to Teague and the safety I felt only with him.

With the promise of a food delivery, Garrick takes his leave, securing us in the bright and delicate set of rooms. Some of the clothes Teague bought for me hang in the closet of the bedroom, the throw I spent so much time wrapped up in is folded across the arm of the sofa. But without Teague here, everything is foreign and uninviting.

I sit in the chair closest to the fire and wait for Winnie to take her seat.

She's a shell of the person who's tended so carefully to me for the past four years. Almost like we've swapped places, back to how we were before…and then some. She almost looks like me.

When she sinks into the corner of the couch and pulls the throw around her, clutching the edge against her mouth as if it will hold back the horror of whatever she's done, I ask, "Tell me what happened."

Tears stream down her face and where I'm calm and strong, she's shaking like a leaf and terrified to give voice to her confession. "It's my fault. I'm the reason they found Teague. Oh my God, Tru, I'm so sorry. If he's hurt… if he's—"

"Don't finish that. Don't give voice to the possibility that he's anything worse than just hurt. Wounds can heal, right? Relationships are forever, so tell me what happened. Who has him?"

Her body shakes with silent sobs, the force required to hold herself together too much to bear. I know that feeling. And I hate that Winnie is experiencing it, but I need her to spill.

"The police. An officer…detective, maybe, was here looking for Teague. Christophe was on a call in his office, so I chatted with him just for a moment. Just for a minute. I was careful, Tru, I was. I know how crooked they are. I know how bad they can be. But he said he was

Teague's cousin and I... I just... Oh my fuck, I'm so fucking sorry. I told him Teague was on his way. That he'd be here soon. He smiled, and I swear I could see the hint of resemblance. I could see that they were related. He said he wouldn't bother us further, that he'd just go meet Teague before he got here and chat with him real quick. I'm so sorry."

Chapter 21

Roar

TEAGUE

I've only been here for a handful of hours, but every single one of them has sucked ass. But the pain coursing through my body hasn't dulled my rage. No, that is fully intact and growing by leaps and bounds.

Every strike striped across my back has me seeing red. Every detail Desmond lays out on the time he spent torturing Truie feeds the murderous fire in my belly. I thought I killed the men who hurt her in the dungeon and thought she took care of the last when she shot Alain. As it turns out, the worst of the monsters escaped unscathed.

That won't stand. If it kills me, if it's the last thing I do, I will rid the world of the worst of the monsters.

"C'mon. You're the one who took her, went all white knight and carried her out, hid her away. How the fuck do you think I'm gonna believe you have no idea? Where the fuck did she hide the fucking thing? It has to be her. She's the one I was fucking. Christ, she made the sweetest sounds when I sliced into her skin, painted her with blood, mixed it with my cum." He grits his teeth in an evil grin as he shares the details like he's an artist proud of his unparalleled masterpiece. "You should have seen her, all red swirled with my pearly white."

I roar. I don't know how I have the energy for it, but I fucking roar before dropping my voice and giving life to all the ways I plan on fucking up his life. "Keep talking, Des. Keep telling me every little detail of the shit you did to that woman, I fucking beg you. Keep talking. Because you, you pencil-dicked little twat... I will rain down on you the same pain, the same torture, the same humiliation, and the same fucking degradation that you so generously bestowed upon her. I will exact her revenge piece by piece, slice by fucking slice."

A telltale whistle through the air warns of the next strike against my back. This one allows the darkness to edge in closer and almost takes me under.

"You can't do shit, Tig. Look at you. Your hands are free and you still can't get yourself out of that chain. Fucking pathetic." He circles me as he taunts. "Maybe you need some motivation. Maybe if I send one of the boys on an errand to catch the little piglet, drag her back here by the fucking toe and give you a front row seat to a show. Maybe then you'll talk. Maybe *she* will. I need that fucking file."

I have never felt so useless, so impotent. Because he's right, my throbbing mangled hands aren't doing me any good. My back is on fire. The only thing sustaining me is the fucking rage.

One hand. If I had use of just one hand, I could do it. Take Desmond down. I'm pretty sure there's only one other guy working with him. Not a cousin, no relation that I know of, and he's young. Fit but inexperienced and maybe not as smart as he should be if he's working with a dirty cop.

The door cracks open, sucking the silence from the room and replacing it with the sounds of classic rock and the garage beyond.

"Uh, boss? There's a guy out here, says he needs to talk to you. Looks official."

Desmond turns, staring at the messenger. "And you think telling me this through an open door is the smart thing to do? Shut the fucking door, you—"

"Hey. You give him the message?" I lift my gaze, the haze clearing as I make eye contact with the floppy-haired kid Christophe seems to have a soft spot for.

Fucking Roux gives me the subtlest of chin lifts. "I need this guy gone, he's blocking the bay, and I can't move the cars out."

"You've got to be fucking kidding me," Desmond growls. "Shut the fucking door. You want to just invite him back here? Who the fuck is it anyway?"

Roux shrugs, wiping his hands on a greasy towel, doing his best to keep his shit tight. And maybe to Desmond, he is, but the little double bounce on his toes and the way his left shoulder shrugs a little higher, a little tighter, has me bracing for the incoming breach.

It happens fast. And quiet.

Roux bobs left and Desmond's sidekick drops in a heap to the floor, blood blooming around him.

Desmond, shitty cop that he is, freezes. Not that there's much he can do. Nowhere he can go.

Christophe's guys, fully kitted in tactical gear, are through the door and on him before he has a chance to react.

"Your kin, right?" Tierney asks, knee in Desmond's back as he holds the blade of his knife to his throat. "You want me to end this for you or...?"

"Jesus, you're a mess." Gaufre pushes through and helps me to stand. Pain lances through my body silencing me. Turning, he adds, "Get Hibou, we're going to need to field dress some of this shit before we can move him." He lifts the chain from around my neck and props me on a metal chair. "I'm gonna hit you with morphine, help dull some of this. You want the cop dead or alive?"

Through gritted teeth and as the needle slides in, I manage, "Don't kill 'im. He's mine," before the drug takes me under.

The world comes back to me in bits and pieces and then a wild rush of panic. I'm prone, lying on what is more massage table than hospital bed, and staring at the floor. I try to lift my head but even that slight movement has my back—both the muscle and skin—screaming in pain. Both hands are heavily bandaged, visible just in my periphery.

"W'ere am I?" I can't see if anyone is in the room with me, but I can't imagine Hibou would leave me completely unattended. "Hey?" My voice is little more than a handful of gravel scraped across a chalkboard. I work my mouth, swallow a pitiful amount of saliva, and try again. "Hey. Where am I?"

"Settle, Grey. You're a fucking mess. Don't need you

undoing all my hard work," Hibou grumbles from somewhere down by my feet. "You're going to be sore for a while, get used to sleeping on your stomach for the next couple of weeks."

"My hands?"

"Yeah. Like I said, a mess. Couple good breaks in one, the wrist of the other. You're lucky you'll be able to piss on your own, but that shake's going to be a challenge. Not going to beat the meat for a while either."

"Jesus."

"Nah, it was all me, buddy. Can't say I got to play God with this one, but it was a fucking miracle I was able to piece you back together. You're welcome."

This fucking guy. He's much more tolerable when I'm upright and intimidating.

"Liked you better when you weren't quite so comfortable running your mouth. Can I sit up? This sucks."

"Eh, not yet. I'm going to give you something for the pain, you'll be out again in no time." Sneaker-clad feet finally make it into my field of view. With them comes a really unwelcome poke to one of the wounds on my upper back. "The worst of it is up here and, you know, your hands, but you're definitely going to want to give this some time."

"Yeah, and that's helping? You should pour salt in

those wounds while you're at it." I mumble the *asshole* under my breath because the last thing I want is him poking and prodding at that shit any more than he already has. "Is Truie safe? Get me Garrick. I need him to check in on her."

He huffs a laugh. "You're timid little pink thing? She's fine, better than fine. Didn't know she had that kind of steel spine in her. Giving orders, standing up to the bossman."

"She what now? What...? Where is she? She's not here," I insist. Wrongly, I should add.

"Pacing her suite like she's got a cleaning list going for Lapin. Raising hell in the quietest way possible." Those sneakers retreat, and I try to raise up again when I get a quick tap to my ribs. "Stay down, tiger, or I'll tie you down myself."

"Get her. Now. Or you won't have a chance to tie shit."

"You sure about this? You've looked a hell of a lot better, man. You want her to see you all fucked up and oozing?"

I don't. But I do need to make sure she's okay. I left her for what was supposed to be a quick meeting, a couple hours of shit I couldn't do from the house, and then I was going straight back to her. Yes, I was going to fuck off work for a bit and get lost in her the way Christophe has with Winnie.

"I need her."

"All right, man. You asked for it." The door opens, and all I hear is mumbling.

"Dude. You have me ass up, feet toward the door? You want to throw a sheet over the lower half or are you trying to shock the shit out of anyone coming in here?"

"Didn't know you were shy, Teague. Nothing to be embarrassed about. It's a little cold in here," he teases, but a sheet lands on my ass, folded low over my back just before the door opens again.

"Is he okay? Will he wake up soon?" Truie asks softly.

"I'm here, hummingbird. I'll be fine soon enough." It's awkward as fuck staring at the floor while talking to her. I would give my left nut to be able to see her big brown eyes. See if she's truly all right.

"Teague." She says my name like a prayer.

There's a light touch to my elbow, my forearm above the cast, before fingers run softly through the hair at the back of my head as knees lower to the ground in front of me.

My eyes fall shut at the sensation. "Not how I expected you to be on your knees for me, hummingbird."

"Right, then," Hibou says from somewhere to my

right. "Let me just pop a little happy juice in your IV, and I'll leave you to it."

A cool tingling spreads through me, and a shiver runs down my spine as the saline flushes the meds through my veins. I don't have much time, and I want to see her, look into Truie's eyes and see for myself that she's as unharmed as she can be.

"I'm going to try to time this. Get just enough pain relief that I can lift up and see your face before I pass out from the drugs."

Before I can brace, Truie's knees slide to the side and then out of my sight, replaced by my folded wool coat. Then the most beautiful gift in the world comes into view as Truie rolls to her back and rests her head on the gray wool like a pillow.

My lips stretch wide, the corners of my mouth lifting into a smile. "Fucking hell, hummingbird. It's good to see your beautiful face smiling up at me."

"You scared me." Her eyes are earnest, her soft smile breaking. "I don't want to feel that again, okay?"

"I don't want you to either. Why didn't you check the tracker? I did that for you, love."

"That's how we found you, but I didn't have a map to overlay. Didn't know you weren't where you were supposed to be until Christophe grabbed my phone."

"And how did you come to be here? I left you safe home for a reason."

"Mm. You went missing. Winnie...W-winnie confirmed that fact and said your boss was pissed. I called Garrick and told him to come get me."

When I open my mouth to protest, she cuts me right off. "I told him I knew why they took you. That I have what they want."

"The file. You took it from Desmond before I pulled you from Alain's dungeon. How?" My brain is getting hazy.

Truie stares at me, likely watching my lights flicker and fade. She reaches up and drags a finger down the side of my face.

Her thumb caresses my lower lip. "When you wake."

Chapter 22

Served

TRUIE

I slept on the floor beneath the table where Teague lay. I waited until he was out, fought like my life depended on it, like the very reason for it was staring down at me. Because he was. And when he finally allowed the drugs to take him to his dreams, I went to mine.

Now that I'm awake, my body aches, and fear stacks on top of worries that are beginning to flare. I have something that very bad people are willing to do very bad things for. I knew that when I was locked away, when the men would come down to the cells and talk about it, speculate what it was, and what they would do if they got ahold of it.

I never thought it would be within my reach.

Never thought I'd have the opportunity to grab it.

That I'd have mere seconds to slide the phone from where it was so carelessly left, that I'd have to dig deep to find the will to move despite the pain, the fear, freaking everything my body had endured that day and for many, many before it.

I knew it was important, that it could potentially save my life, and if karma was truly a thing, it could ruin the lives of those who had fucked mine up so badly. I didn't know what I was going to do with it, only that I had to keep it hidden and pray that no one connected me to its disappearance.

To feel a familiarity years later, to recognize Teague's soul as if I'd known it for half of a lifetime, to fall irrefutably in love with a man I only knew from the shadows of my dreams was not what I anticipated.

As carefully and quietly as I can manage, I roll to my side and push to standing. I barely manage to swallow down the startled screech at seeing Christophe looming in the open doorway.

He stares at the stripes raised across his friend's back, almost like he's inventorying each and every one of them to make sure retribution is properly and appropriately served. His intensity has had me on edge since the day of the funerals, but I've compartmentalized as much as possible since he saved Winnie. Now though, now his focus seems like maybe it could be a good thing.

I don't know who to trust with the full weight of my secret. But the bits I gave to Garrick helped to save Teague, and Christophe most definitely looks as though he's fully prepared to match energy, strike for strike.

When he finally lifts his gaze from the devastation that is Teague's back and meets my eye, I've steeled my spine. He lifts his chin and stalks from the room, knowing I'll fall in line and follow him. Christophe has things to say.

"Tell me what you know about *le livret*." His voice is softer, kinder than I've heard toward anyone other than Winnie, but I'm not French enough to speak the language.

"I don't know what you're talking about." I do, mostly, but doing this, completely on my own, is scary.

"The journal, my uncle called it. He had it, wanted it back bad enough to make some very poor choices with my honeybee."

"Worse than he'd ever done," a very familiar and very shouldn't-be-out-of-bed voice says from behind me.

I whip around and am halfway to standing when Teague continues, "Sit, hummingbird. We need to know what we're dealing with."

"B-but your back?" Super proud that only one of those words stuck.

I watch closely as he lowers himself into the chair next to me, catching himself before he leans into the back of it. He tries to lean forward, elbows on his knees, but with the bandage and cast, that's not really a good position either.

"You should still be in bed, asleep." My brows knit together, and I have to hold myself back from flitting and fussing all around him.

The doctor appears in the doorway of the office. "Yeah, you fucking should. You need to rest, stay still to give your back a chance to mend."

Teague rolls his eyes and addresses him over his should. "Not going to happen. We have shit to see to and not time enough to do it. Make yourself useful and get Eddie over here."

"You want me to tell Eddie what to do? Right, like that'll work."

Christophe's voice is sharp when he says, "Hibou, do it. Tell Edmond his presence is required and then go home. I'm sure Miss Cochonette will take very good care of your patient. If we need you, we'll call." And just like that, the doctor is effectively dismissed.

With Teague here, I feel better, almost relieved at

the thought of giving up everything I've been hiding. "It's not a journal, more of a file."

"Wait," Christophe commands, the harsh edge very much back in his voice. And for an odd amount of time, we do. After the distant sounds of the front door closing echoes in the entry way, Christophe nods.

"What was—"

He leans back in his massive chair—almost a throne—and crosses his ankle over the opposite knee, the picture of zero fucks given. "I thought this might hold some aspects of a personal nature. For your benefit, I felt it best to have as few ears as possible in the vicinity."

Christophe's consideration is a surprise, a welcome one, because I hadn't even thought of that. My focus was solely on unburdening myself and keeping anyone else from suffering through what Teague had.

"Thank you. That was…"

"It was necessary," he finishes, softly but firmly.

Garrick enters the office bearing a silver coffee service among other things. "Pardon the interruption," he says as he settles the tray and begins work preparing cups of coffee for Christophe and I. "Electrolytes and a bottle of water for you, Mr. Grey. Mr. Yore will be here shortly. Is there anything further?" Without waiting for a response, he sets a small tray of sweet treats on the desk in front of me.

"No. Thank you. When Eddie gets here, send him right in, please." Christophe sips his black coffee, allowing his eyes a slow blink in appreciation before he settles his gaze on me, right back in business mode. "Go ahead, Tru."

So I do. I tell the two men about how I stole one of my captor's phones. How he'd unloaded the pockets of his jeans, setting keys, phones, wallet, and weapon on the table just outside the cell I was held in.

My hands start trembling as the words tumble from my lips, and I have to place my cup on the edge of Christophe's desk, so I don't spill its contents.

Teague reaches out to take my hand, pausing with his casted wrist hovering in the space between us. He places it back on the armrest of his chair and mumbles "Fucking Desmond" under his breath. The bounce of his knee that's always present grows until his whole body is practically vibrating.

Before continuing, I stand, slide my chair right next to his, and take my place, sitting cross-legged, my hand hooked gently around the crook of his arm. The contact seems to calm his wild. And maybe mine too.

"He... When he was there... doing the things he, um, h-he liked to do to me..." Giving voice to the things I experienced is harder than I imagined it would be. Even when I was in therapy, I struggled to say exactly what was done.

"You don't have to share that if you don't want," Teague says, his focus dancing between Christophe and me. "Not everyone needs all of the details—you control those very private ones."

I lean over and press my lips to the rounded muscle of his shoulder and then rest my forehead there while I think about what to say next.

"That was the day—the last one there. There was a scuffle, banging around at the end of the hall and he, the man, stopped what he was doing to me and grabbed his things and ran down the hall. Away from the noises. I, um, I-I-I... a phone dropped. It was on the floor by the cell, and I crawled off the cot to it and grabbed it. Folded my hands around it and closed my eyes, waiting."

"For me," Teague adds.

"For you." I kiss his shoulder again and then straighten in my chair, the hardest part over. "It was an older phone, smaller than the one you gave me, I was able to keep it hidden. Deep inside, my heart hinted that I was safe with you, but my world, my whole fucking world had been turned upside down and stolen by the person who was supposed to keep me safe. I-I-I didn't know who to trust, so I kept the phone hidden. It went under a loose floorboard in the back of Winnie's closet when I went away—to the hospital," I clarify. There were too many times I just *went away* or *disappeared* to keep track of.

"When I was released, I had nowhere else to go, so Winnie took me in. Took care of me and kept me as safe as she could but I was broken. So broken." Tears gather and instead of fighting it, I let them fall. In all that's happened in the past few weeks, I've come to feel comfortable enough to let down some of my walls, safe with Teague right here.

"Bent, hummingbird. Never broken." Through a stoic grimace of pain, Teague manipulates me out of my chair and into his lap, his arms wrapped carefully around me. Lips pressed to the crown of my head, he says, "At your pace, love, remember that. You're in control."

"I was terrified living under the same roof as Henri and Claudette. Their big parties had pretty much fizzled, but there were still people, scary people, in and out of the house all the time. I hid a lot. Moved the phone a lot. Kept it close, easy to access, but hidden away, always.

"You were there when they died," I say pointedly to Christophe, then turn my attention to Teague recounting what we'd already discussed. "And you." The number of times I've thought about that but didn't give voice to it is a lot. *A lot* a lot. "I wasn't scared, though. Never when you came to see them—I knew I was okay when you were there. But when I came down the stairs and saw that they were dead, I froze. For years, I lived in a house with known users and dealers, and the police never showed their faces. But with dead bodies, there wasn't a choice.

"I grabbed the phone, sat on the stairs, and waited for Winnie. I went to the place in my mind where I escaped when they did the things they did to me. My darkness."

"Where is it now?"

I startle at the new voice, muscles going tight and Teague grunts as I burrow deeper into his safety. Caught between hiding and worry at hurting Teague even more, I still, whispering *I'm sorry, I'm sorry* over and over and over again.

"Fucking hell, Eddie. You couldn't announce yourself?"

"Christophe knew I was here."

"He's not the one with traumatic anxiety, asshole."

"Is that what you think? God, I've even got you fooled." Christophe winks at me, a small smile tipping his lips, and dips his chin. "Eddie is our legal counsel. Client privilege is in effect so you're safe here," he promises.

"When Winn called the police, I left. I went to the woods, popped the SIM card from the phone and threw that into the woods."

"And the SIM card?" the lawyer asks.

"I hid it."

"Out there? In this weather?" He scowls and curls his lips. "It's most likely corrupted as fuck. Useless after being exposed to dirt and the cold and rain."

"It… I bagged it."

"What?"

I lift my head, sitting straight and feeling brave surrounded by Teague, and stare over his shoulder at the man sitting in the same chair Winnie had occupied just the day before.

"I lived in a house where drugs were sold and consumed at a stupid volume. Small bags were literally everywhere. The card is dry."

Eddie stares back at me, brows high, eyes wide, chin tucked. Maybe I should be offended that he's surprised at my forethought, at my resourcefulness, but, God, I just don't have it in me. I still have bigger things to worry about.

"Good girl," Teague murmurs, drawing my focus back to him. His eyes are pinched, his face pale. "And where did you stash it, hummingbird?"

And just like that, the last of my secrets comes tumbling out. "In our journal. In the tree."

Chapter 23

Treasures

TEAGUE

Her strength.

The quiet strength Truie possesses astounds me.

I'm not surprised at the steps she took to snag and safeguard information that she thought—knew—was bigger than her. And not really bothered that she didn't spill, give it all up to me as soon as she started feeling safe with me.

No, the thing that kicks my ass is that it was here all along. First, in my pocket when I found her. I kept it safe when Hibou looked her over and tucked it back in her hand when I dropped her at Winnie's front door. I don't know why I did that; it wasn't like I thought for an instant that it was hers, but she'd held it so tightly in her hand, and I couldn't fathom taking one more thing from her after all she'd been through.

And then, it was literally a stone's throw away. Just outside, not fifty yards from where we're sitting right fucking now.

Christophe and Eddie rise and wordlessly leave the room, going out to find the tree, no doubt.

"I am so fucking proud of you, hummingbird." I lift her chin so I can see her eyes. This whole thing has been a lot. "You're stronger than anyone I know. So fucking proud of you."

I search her eyes and swipe at the trail of tears on her cheek with the back of my fingers what little peeks out from the black cast immobilizing my wrist. I press my mouth to hers and sweep my tongue along the seam of her lips.

When Desmond was beating the shit out of me, I had a moment where I thought I'd never get to do this again. Never taste her. Never feel her sweet body pressed to mine.

And here she fucking is, in my useless arms. Jesus, I'm out of commission for the foreseeable future, like a baby who can't do shit for himself.

I pour myself into the kiss, stroking her tongue with mine, tasting her. Owning her the only way I can right now. I would give my left nut to be able to touch her, run my fingers over every inch of her body and make her mine.

I roll my hips, my dick hard against her sweet ass. Truie slides her hands over my shoulders, twisting her fingers in my hair. I want to get closer to her, need to, so I lean back and thrust my hips and screech like a little bitch.

"Oh," Truie yelps, jumping off my lap at the same time Christophe and Eddie waltz back into the room.

Christophe glares at me while addressing Truie, "If he hurt you, I'll finish the job Des started."

Red paints Truie's cheeks as she shakes her head adamantly. "N-no, I think it was me. I hurt him. God, Teague, is your back okay? Did any of the scabs tear?"

"Pretty sure he'd be willing to lay down on a bed of broken glass and then some for you." Eddie rolls his eyes and settles into Christophe's chair, pulling the laptop in front of him. He attaches a card reader to one of the side ports and extracts a SIM card from multiple small zip lock bags.

Ignoring the tension hanging thick and heavy in the office, he slides the card into the reader and mumbles, "Here we go. Probably won't be able to get anything worth a shit." He taps on the touchpad and waits, Christophe posted up behind him while I sit across the desk from them, staring at Truie, with a hard on I can't do a single thing with. Fucking awkward as hell is what this is.

I should move, peel my back off of the leather chair and pray that I don't leave all my DNA behind, but I'm terrified. I don't think I can handle making that noise again.

"Huh. Would you fucking look at that," Eddie mumbles.

Christophe leans in and huffs a laugh. "Jesus, fuck." He shifts his gaze to Truie as Eddie scrolls through the information and adds, "Looks like you did it. There's... God damn, there's fucking everything here, enough to ruin pretty much everyone in this town. What do you want to do with it?"

Truie steps away from the desk and freezes. "Me?"

"You. This is here because you took care, protected it, guarded it with your life. What happens now is up to you." Christophe and I have talked, he knows at least to some degree how much of Truie's control was stripped away from her. I owe him for keeping that in mind as he holds what could likely end him in the palm of his hand.

"What if...what if I don't want to make that decision? What if I don't want anything to do with it anymore?"

"Then that's your choice, hummingbird." I reach to

take her hand, again, and can't. "Fucking Desmond needs to pay for all the shit he did to us." I growl, loud and full of frustration as I lean forward, peeling my back from the leather. When I stand, Truie's wedged between Christophe's desk and me. I wrap my arms around her, looking at my boss and his lawyer, whose head is likely spinning at all the dirty deeds he can no longer deny knowledge of. "We done here? I need to lay down and—"

"Before you fall down. Probably pretty light-headed about now," Eddie finishes without even shifting his focus.

"Go. You've earned your day off"—Christophe redirects his focus from me to Truie—"I promise to safeguard this for you—"

"It's yours. I don't want it. I don't want the details of what it says, or what you do with it. I want to put all of that behind me as much as I can."

"You have my word. But make things right with my wife. She's devastated, and I can't stand for that to continue. She made a mistake, a big one for sure, but she needs to be absolved. Talk to her."

"I will."

One small hand presses into my abdomen, turning me toward the exit from the room. We walk side by side to my suite, silence rife with so many questions, I'm not sure where to start, or if I even want to. I could sleep for a week.

Truie stops in the hallway between my suite and the one that was supposed to be hers. She presses her thumb to the panel next to my door, releasing the lock and opening it for me. I step through surprised when she doesn't immediately follow me.

"I think Winnie's in there"—her gaze slides to the open door across the hall—"I'm going to talk to her. Go ahead and try to get comfortable, I'll be right in."

I stay exactly where I am. I'd cross my arms over my chest to emphasize the fact that I'm not taking my eyes off of her, but the action would be comical at best. Big, bad-ass, ginger only goes so far on a good day. With my hands wrapped, casted and basically useless, I'm fairly certain I'd come off more like a helpless kitten than anything else. But I hold my ground and watch her slip into the room, listen to the gently whispered words and the soft sobs. And when the women exit the room, hand in hand, I take stock of Truie, confirming that whatever just happened inside that room didn't leave her with any more scars.

Winnie stifles a gasp when she sees me, gaze hitting each of my hands, and the marks on my face. "I'm so sorry, Teague. I'm so—"

"No worries," I tell her, extending my wrapped

broken hand toward Truie. "Help me get settled, hummingbird. I'm about dead on my feet."

Truie gives Winnie's hand a quick squeeze and release then enters my suite.

"You really love her," Winnie says, softly. Reverently.

"More than my own life," I respond, noting the sob as I turn on my heel giving her an unobstructed view of my back and let the door swing shut behind me.

"You l-love me?"

"God, yes. I fucking do. A lot."

"Even though it was my fault you got hurt?"

The fact that I can laugh at all should more than make up for my lack of...fucking something, I don't know. I hurt all over and want nothing more than to fall into bed and bury myself in Truie's body and fuck away the past day and a half. But again, I fucking hurt.

"No part of that was your fault. My cousin has been toeing the line for longer than he ever should have been allowed to. He got one up on me this time, but it'll be the last. He's right and truly fucked now." I take slow, careful steps toward the bedroom. "Will you come with me? Comfort me while I think of all the ways I want to kill him?"

"You-you're kidding, right?" she asks picking up a basket of bandages and bottles and follows me.

"I'm not. He hurt me, tried to make it so I'd be useless to protect you and ran his mouth the entire fucking time he did. He was going to go after you next to get what he wanted. He deserves much worse than death."

Weary, hurting, and frustrated as hell, I sit on the bench at the foot of my bed. If we were at my house, I'd happily grit my way through the pain, scream as needed, and show this woman just exactly how much I love her. Make her come over and over and over again until the only reason she has trouble forming words is because her synapses are in full meltdown.

Her basket in tow, Truie sits on the mattress behind me, legs loose on either side of my hips. Like she's handling a fragile treasure, she tends to each of the wounds on my back, cleaning up any evidence of my mishap with leaning against the leather, unprotected.

"What's that?" I ask as a thin film adheres to the stripes highest on my shoulder.

"The film tattoo artists use for healing?" Truie sounds like she's reading that straight from a packaging.

"Where'd you get that?" I twist to see just what this magic basket contains, and it is indeed packets and packets of derma film, instant ice packs, and enough ibuprofen to choke a horse.

"The note says to dress the wounds on your back, ice

your hands, and take ibuprofen as needed but the pain pills if you're being a pain in *my* ass." She works as she shares that tidbit and soon, my skin is covered with swaths of the thin film. And it feels somehow better. Like it won't rip open and stick to the sheets or a shirt. Like I can lie on my back.

My eyes widen as hope surges and blood rushes straight to my dick. "Does it say who left this basket of treasures?" I turn to face Truie, scanning the mess scattered across the foot of the bed. She tilts the notecard so I can see that there is in fact no name, simply a stylized drawing of a rabbit. "Nice."

"Does this mean anything to you?" she asks gathering the trash into a neat pile.

"It means the world to me." I take Truie's mouth and kiss her until she's panting and breathless.

She pulls back just enough for her words to fill the space between our lips. "I think you should lay down. You-you've had a big day and..." She rolls her lips between her teeth, her tongue darting out to swipe a delicious path across her lush pink mouth.

"And what?" I stand and move to the side of the bed, looming over her, the scrub pants I grabbed before wandering down to Christophe's office hiding not one bit of my intentions.

"Maybe you should... let me take care of you." She

shifts on her knees until she's facing me, and that fucking lip is back between her teeth.

"Is that what you want, hummingbird? To take care of me?"

Her chin dips, and I swear to all that's holy, there's a fucking sparkle in her eye as she pulls at my drawstring. My pants slide down, pooling at my feet and Truie shuffles backward, making room for me.

She looks so beautiful kneeling in the center of my bed, cheeks flushed, eyes wide. Pupils blown. She's a fucking vision.

I hate that I'm so limited, but I climb onto the bed, my back resting against the pile of pillows by the headboard. Gently, carefully, I shift down a little on the mattress, hips canted, knees bent. Useless fucking hands resting out to the sides.

And Truie Cochonette does just that—takes care of me—in the best way possible.

Chapter 24

Exertion

TEAGUE

The fact that I dragged my ass out of bed today shows just how dedicated I am to my job.

Pfft. Who am I kidding, this one is all for the soft, pliant woman in my bed. But I have to deal with Desmond and the sooner I have him taken care of, the better. All Christophe said was to make him go away. How I make that happen is entirely in my hands. So to speak.

"Where are you going?" Truie's sleepy voice is hushed and sexy. Makes me want to just say fuck it all. I can't think of a better way to spend my morning, my entire day, than buried between her thighs. Maybe lying on my back with her sitting on my face but standing here trying to figure out how to get dressed with limited use of my hands is just shitty.

"I have some things I need to take care of. Think you can help me?" Jesus, did I mention this is shitty? The goal for so long was to be taking our clothes off, never, never for her to be helping me put them back on.

"Mm. You should be resting so you can heal. You shouldn't exert yourself." She blinks up at me sleepily, and I feel even worse about needing her help. But the alternative is to walk through the estate until I find Garrick or someone else to help me with my boxers.

Fucking bullshit.

I lean down, bracketing her face with my elbows and take her mouth, tasting and kissing her breathless. I don't want to go, don't want to leave this room at all.

That Truie is on board with this is obvious as her arms wind around my neck and her fingers sift through my hair, tugging hard and holding me close.

Little by little I slow the kissing, pull back to brush my words against her lips. "You didn't think I exerted myself last night? Didn't I give you what you were after while you were riding my cock?" I press my hips against her because I could easily go again and remind of just how hard she came. "I didn't hear you telling me to rest while I was deep inside you. Didn't hear you telling me to take it easy… and not exert myself."

Her palm slides between us, landing in the center of my chest. She pushes me back as she sits up, hair a tousled mess, warm and sleepy but that sparkle in her coffee-colored eyes that's her tell.

Her hands skate down my abs and curl around my cock, stroking, toying, playing. "You should let others cater to you until you're healed." Her tongue darts out, licking my tip, before she slides her luscious lips around me.

"Fuck, hummingbird" My head falls back as she works my dick. Slow and soft, hard and fast, all of it fucking life affirming.

It takes an embarrassingly short amount of time for her to make me come, but when she licks the last of my cum from her lips, a switch flips, and she's all business.

A quick shower, my woman on her knees in front of me, her fingers tickling and teasing as she dresses me like I'm a fucking child and I am right back to a hard dick that I truly can't do anything about. Trapped behind my belt, buttons, and zipper, my cock is likely not seeing the light of day until this shit with my cousin is done and put to rest.

Fucking stupid bullshit.

Makes me that much more angry and ready to take my frustrations out on the bastard.

"Go back to sleep, hummingbird. I'll be back as soon

as I'm done and then I can fuck you again." I tuck Truie back into bed, and kiss her thoroughly, the promise of what's to come imbued in every thrust of my tongue.

Getting out of my suite is fine, but as the door clicks behind me, I realize just how badly getting back in is going to suck without the use of my hands.

The inconvenience, the pain, fucking all of that simmers as I make my way to the entryway where McGill is waiting. Doors open and close behind me as I get ushered from the house, to the SUV, to the warehouse, and down into the workroom.

The insulation on the ceiling is soundproof, though we are so far away from any functional warehouses, no one knows what goes on down here. Christophe has generally kept it free of occupants, choosing to do more of his business above board, but today is special. After all, Desmond is *family*.

And the man of the hour is stripped down to his boxers and balancing on his knees, chain around his neck, hands cuffed behind him.

I believe in poetry, strongly when it's applied to justice, so it's not lost on me the similarities in his position and how he had me. Gaufre does good work.

I drop into the large leather desk chair that was brought down here just for me. Because I might talk a good game, but I'm wiped. Any energy I can save is going straight into reserve for Truie.

Desmond watches as I ease myself back into the chair, feet wide, elbows slung casually on each of the armrests.

Seconds tick by, silent and weighted, until the drop of self-preservation hits.

"Cousin, Tig, let me go. Please don't... don't do this, man."

He spins himself so he's facing me head-on, balancing on knees that just barely touch the floor. His neck straining where the chain holds his back straight and his chin tall. He looks pitiful.

I could feel bad. I could show him some mercy.

But I don't.

"Some nerve, asking me for leniency, Des. Some fucking nerve." My tone is calm, detached. Almost dispassionate, though passion is the driving force behind this.

"W-we're family. You... you... Look man, I didn't have a choice. I had to take you and—"

"Bullshit."

"What? No, I'm... I didn't mean—"

"Bullshit, again." I take my time staring at him, spinning up his mind and wearing down his resolve.

Time stretches, and the strain of waiting shows in the way his shoulders tremble and shake.

He opens his mouth, but I cut him off before he gets started. "You had a choice." This is my show even if I'm only a spectator and can't join in for any actual fun.

"No, I—"

"You had a fucking choice, Des, and you made really piss-poor ones."

"I'm sorry. I'm sorry, I swear. Let me go and I'll never bother you again. Never—"

"And the only way to learn the lesson here is biblical. An eye-for-an-eye, you know?"

Desmond sighs, relief settling in his shoulders. "Thank Christ. I-I can do that." His head bounces in a series of short nods. He's obviously talking himself into this. "One for one."

I cock my head and relax into the chair, tilting the seat back so I can get comfortable for watching this show. "We'll start with that," I tell him, then turn to address Gaufre. "Might want to suit up, this is going to get messy."

Christophe's enforcer shakes out a pair of Tyvek coveralls and shoves his feet into the pant legs. "On it," he grumbles.

The man is serious about his work, and this project is special to him. Not for personal reasons, but because he prefers to stay underground, out of sight, and saving my sorry ass required him to come up out of his hideaway.

"What do you... You don't need that, right, Tig? He doesn't need...*fuck*." Desmond swears under his breath as Gaufre zips his clean suit and flips the hood up to cover his hair.

He pulls a blade from the table and tests the edge, asking, "You got a count for me?"

Do I fucking ever.

I spent a lot of time between Truie's thighs last night. Sure, I fucked her good, but I also counted. Every single cut was kissed and cataloged, accounted for so the strict adherence to the Code of Hammurabi could be met. Every slice in Truie's skin will be scored into Desmond's, that's our first order of business.

I give Gaufre the number. "Might want to grab a second blade, I don't have all day."

Desmond stiffens. "What? I never cut you, man. Actually, I didn't do nothin'. Never laid a finger on you, that was the kid and..."

I laugh. "You don't get it."

"No. I fucking don't." Panic rings high in his voice. "Hit me. Slash at me, break my fucking hands. That sure as fuck won't take all day. And if you had a proper drain in the floor for your wet work—"

As he's flapping his gums, I lift my chin to Gaufre

and give him the go ahead to get started. The first handful of cuts are clean, the skin fresh, so the pain doesn't hit immediately. But when it does, Desmond stops his blathering and swears.

"Again," I say, not giving him any time to recover.

Gaufre works quickly, adding to his canvas every time I mutter *Again*.

With each series of cuts, I remind my cousin of the shit he did. Of all his heinous deeds. Of the way he touched my woman when he had no fucking right.

I keep the panic she felt at the forefront.

The constant fear.

The filth and neglect she suffered over the months she was in his grips.

And he just whines and whimpers like the piece of shit he is. She was there because her father gave her up to Alain, and that bastard was more than happy to keep her tucked away in the dark. But they're gone and retribution still has to be served. So here we are.

The numbers are adding up, but Desmond's sagging, exhausted from the constant bite of pain, and probably from the way I've recounted all the horrible things he did to Truie. His thighs are a mess of blood, the skin peeling back. "Looks like shit," Gaufre observes as Desmond pants and moans. "I take pride in my work, Teague. This is sloppy. Fucking amateur looking."

He glances at me over his shoulder, his blade paused in its arc.

"Yeah. Honestly, I'm getting bored." I shrug, the stripes on my shoulder tugging from the beat-down Desmond granted me. My knee bounces as I stare at the bloody mess, weighing how much time and effort he's worth. I've been away from Truie for a couple of hours, and that's long enough for me.

I push to my feet and walk to the edge of the blood splatter, careful not to step over the line.

"You done or you want to keep playing?" I direct the question to Gaufre but keep a close eye on Desmond and the way he's sagging in his restraints.

Gaufre shrugs like he hasn't just flayed open a man's thighs. "I could keep at it. Got nothing else to do today."

I nod and retreat a step. "You do what makes you happy. I'm going home to my hummingbird. Hibou send drugs in case you need to revive him?"

"Yeah. Didn't look too happy when he saw my worktable and this fucker strung up ready to be gutted. I'd watch him if I were you."

I file that away and stalk to the door, kicking at the steel with the toe of my boot since my hands are fucking useless.

"Teague?" Desmond croaks weakly. "When I get out of here—"

"You're not leaving, not in one piece, a body bag, though, if there are enough pieces to warrant one."

"But eye for an eye. I didn't kill you or the little bitch."

Is he really trying to negotiate with me? Now? Hanging from a chain with the skin falling off his thighs?

"That rule was for the courts, Des, not individuals. You should have paid closer attention."

The steel door swings shut behind me, dropping us into a perfect silence that is fucking beautiful.

"You clean up after yourself?" Eddie barks from the depths of Christophe's office.

I bend my elbows and hold my pristine bandaged hands up in front of me like I'm a surgeon who's just scrubbed in. "We hire that shit done."

"Fucking asshole," he mumbles. "You gonna have Jess there for hours cleaning up after you."

"Not my problem, man." I drop my hands and pop my shoulder up. "You finally gonna tap that? That why you're pissy?"

Eddie grumbles some more about the mess that

needs to be cleaned, but I tune him out and stalk down the hallway, erasing the space between Truie and me.

Now that I finally have her, I can't get enough. Doesn't matter how bad my hands ache or my back burns, the best balm for my ailments is hummingbird kisses.

And I'm going up to lose myself in her.

Chapter 25

Dirty

TRUIE

I drop to my knees, landing with an *oof* to the soft ground. Moisture seeps through the knees of my deep berry overalls, chilling my skin and sending a shiver up my spine.

I dig my fingers deep into the rich brown soil and push it to the side.

The warm breeze stills for a moment and as a shadow moves across me, casting me into darkness the calming scent swirls around me.

"Love seeing you dirty and on your knees, hummingbird."

I rock back, sitting on my heels with my hands folded on top of my thighs. They're filthy, dirt etched into my skin and packed under my nails from digging in my hummingbird garden. I spent the cold months of winter planning the flowers, the varieties, the ones that have the sweetest nectar and draw the tiny birds in, the ones that nourish them and make them strong. I couldn't be happier.

I tilt my head back, gazing up, up, up until all I see is the sun streaming through Teague's hair, haloing the auburn waves in an angelic glow. His face is in shadow. I can't see his smile, but I know it's there.

He takes one step closer, then another until the tips of his boots bracket my knees. I shift to the left and forward, my forehead resting on his muscular thigh. And when he drops his warm palm to the back of my head, another shiver trails down my spine.

Teague spent a full month recovering from the damage done to his hands. There wasn't a lot to keep him occupied and there were times he was more of a caged tiger than a man. The skin on his back healed quickly enough, though the scars that streak the broad planes of muscle rival my own. But there wasn't a lot that held his attention during the dark days of winter. Other than me.

"You're home earlier than I thought you'd be."

"Yeah? You have something special planned?" he

says, voice low and full of gravel. "Can I entice you to come inside and get dirty with me?"

I sit back again and meet his heated gaze. "I'm caked in dirt. You want to join me here?"

"Mm. Didn't think you'd want to risk your pretty flowers, but I will gladly roll around in the garden with you." He tosses his phone and keys to the side and drops to his knees, pushing me off balance. He pins me down and takes my mouth, licking inside and sucking on my tongue.

I hold my hands out to the sides, careful not to smear his white linen shirt with mud.

"Hummingbird, you okay?" He pulls back just enough to meet my gaze, concern pushing his brows low.

I nod, matching his concern with my own. "Why?"

"You're not touching me. Did I scare you? Was I too aggressive?" He's hovering over me, the angle just different enough that his face is no longer in shadow.

The only places he's touching me are where his knees bracket mine and his hands cradling my head.

"I-I'm perfect. I just didn't want to get you dirty." I flick my gaze to my hand and then back to him. "Your shirt is so...so white."

"All I want is to get dirty with you. The dirtier, the better." He glances over my head, mapping the yard with his eyes, noting just how exposed we are in this moment. "But maybe we should take this inside. I don't want the cameras picking up anything no one else should see."

He plants his hands to the sides of my head and pushes up, hopping to his feet at the same time.

Before I can do much more than push up on my elbows, he reaches down and scoops me up, tossing me over his shoulder like a sack of potatoes.

"Put me down," I screech, kicking my legs.

He wraps his arms around them, holding me tight while bounding across the yard. "Hold on, baby, I don't want to hurt you."

"But your shirt..."

"Fuck my shirt. I've plenty more."

"B-but, they're expensive. R-real l-l-linen." The stuttering is strictly tied to the way I'm bouncing on the round of his shoulder.

Since we've sequestered ourselves away here, I haven't fought with my words more than a handful of times. Teague calms me. Centers me.

Teague bounds up the stairs, and I have no choice but to hold on for my dear life. He slides me down his front so I feel every hard ridge of him as I go. He cages me in as he presses his palm to the door, allowing us access to the house.

I stumble through the doorway. Teague follows,

slamming the door closed behind him, turning to hit the extra deadbolt as if anyone could get through his security system as it is. And of course, right in the center of his back, two brown splotches of mud mar the pristine white of his dress shirt.

I sink, curling into myself at the mess I made. More often than not, I don't worry about upsetting Teague, he's shown me over and over again that he's not interested in that. But this time it hits me. And I can't explain why…it just does.

"Oh, hummingbird, no." Teague croons, soothing my rough edges. "No tears. Not over a scrap of fabric." He pops the buttons at his cuffs and three at his neck and then reaches behind his head and pulls the shirt free from his body. Muscles ripple. Light dances in the shadows of each dip and valley, abs bunching, and shoulders rolling forward as he crouches down into my space.

I flinch.

His proximity isn't the problem. There really isn't a problem except I'm stuck in the nonsensical loop of dirt on a shirt.

We've spent so much time here, away from the world, tucked into our quiet and the simplicity of our new lives, that my freakout is kind of freaking me out.

Gentle hands guide me to the sink, lathering my hands and scrubbing the dirt away until the water runs clear. Once dry, Teague hold them together, between his palms.

The Celtic cross over his heart, frames my clasped hands and slowly, when my breaths are even again, and matching Teague's in pace and depth, I relax. I let go of the last strains of panic and press a kiss to where his hands cover mine.

"I'm sorry," I say, pausing to make sure my words don't fuck me over again. "I don't know what that was."

"Doesn't matter. You're good now, though?" He's so steady, so staid and soothing.

I nod, a handful of tiny movements, and then tilt my face to his, gaze catching on the distinct pucker of derma film. "What happened? Turn around, Teague. Turn around, quick." I pull my hands from his and push at him, trying to turn that big body with not an ounce of luck.

He huffs a laugh, as relaxed as can be. "Calm down, hummingbird."

My head snaps and, for a brief moment, I go completely still. But this isn't the time for me to fall apart, so I steel my spine and shake off whatever isn't helping in this moment. My chest expands as I suck in a big breath. I don't know where the strength comes from or if he just gives in, but I manage to turn Teague enough to see the thin plastic film is covering fresh red.

I wobble, feeling woozy, and very much not stable. "Wh-what...? That..."

Finally, Teague turns fully, the back of his left shoulder on display.

And the artwork is breathtaking.

"I don't... That's..."

"You. It's you, hummingbird."

And it is. Nestled in the scars that stripe his back is a hummingbird, ruby-red throat, black head, gray and white body, dancing in the air. Surrounding it are hundreds of small red blooms perched on stems made of his scars.

It's stunning. Beauty from ruin.

"When... Why?" I can't get a complete thought to form. I'm okay but rattled.

Stunned.

Honored.

"Today. I wanted you close, always." He turns back to me again, cupping my face between his calloused palms. "Already had the cross over my heart, but with you at my back, my heart can rest safe and sure. Always. Need you in my life, Truie. Always."

"I, Teague, I..." A laugh bubbles up from deep inside me, erupting on a breath. "You literally have me chipped."

"Don't start that."

"Like a dog."

"Truie," he warns, but there's no bite.

"A dog."

"And you have me tagged as well."

He's not wrong. I check on him several times a day when he's away from me. But this is different. "You had me etched into your skin. That's…"

"It's fucking beautiful. And I'd do it again. A hundred times over."

I step behind him and trace the scars, the lines, the flowers. The bird perfectly still but in constant motion suspended in midair. I press a kiss to the edge of the protective film. And then to the center of his back and wrap my arms tightly around his waist, tears stinging at the corners of my eyes.

"Thank you." I kiss him again before he swings an arm around and pulls me to his front. "Thank you for saving me"

"You saved yourself."

"Thank you for loving me."

"There's nothing to thank there."

"Thank you for bringing me out of the darkness."

I press my lips to his, swallowing his words and drinking them in.

Overalls may very well be the least alluring clothing, but they are convenient. I unclip the straps and let them fall, pooling at my feet. Fumbling, I do away with his belt, the buttons, the zipper, shoving his pants and briefs down and away like they've personally offended me.

Teague walks right out of them and strides across the room to our favorite chair in front of the fireplace. "Want you too bad. Need you now." He sits, settling my ass on his spread thighs.

When his fingers find me wet and ready, he grumbles, "Hold on, hummingbird," positioning me just where he needs me, he thrusts, filling me all at once. "Fuck, yes. You ready?"

I nod and reach for his shoulders.

Teague grips my hips, moving me up and down as he thrusts into me. Bouncing me on his lap.

It's quick.

It's dirty.

And it's absolutely perfect.

He fucks me in the chair, on the stairs. In the hallway outside our bedroom. Doing as he promised and dirtying me up before he runs us a bath and pulls me in with him, settling me between his thighs.

I melt into him as his arms circle me—one nestled between my breasts logging each time my heart beats, solely for him. The other traces the scars that line my thighs.

"I love these."

I turn my head to meet his lazy gaze. "My scars?"

"Every one of them," he says. "They're a part of you. The marks that show your strength. Without them you wouldn't be you. And I don't want to live in a world without you in it, Truie. Say you'll stay with me always."

It's the easiest word I've ever said.

No pausing.

No counting.

No stuttering.

"Always."

Chapter 26

...because what good is the Hundred Acre Woods without Rabbit and Eeyore?

JESSALINE LAPIN

"For the love of all things good and holy, what—and I do mean this with all sincerity—the fuck?" I nudge the barely recognizable body with the toe of my favorite boot. "Why didn't you give me the heads up to change into work clothes?"

I twist an earbud into my ear and shove my phone into my back pocket. It's not like I don't have a cleaning kit in my car at all times but man, I literally just got these boots broken in and comfortable.

An exasperated sigh tickles my ear, sending a burst of electricity down my spine. It shouldn't be a thrill. Shouldn't set my soul on fire and make my panties an inefficacious mess.

But it does.

That sigh, the utter exasperation it embodies, the man who literally breathes life into it has me tied up in knots. And the more he sighs, the more he sinks into his head, the deeper he goes into his void, the more I want to do whatever it takes to free him of the dark cloud he thinks is his constant companion.

"Can you help me out here or not?"

I stop and let my eyes drift closed, my mind swirling and dancing with the possibilities, all the ways I'd like to give him a hand. Most of them *not* what he's asking about.

"Have I ever left you hanging, Eddie?"

And there it is again…

…that fucking sigh.

Thank you for choosing to spend time in this wild reimagining of the Hundred Acre Woods. Who could have ever guessed that after Christophe and Winnie, we'd be here ruminating on Teague and Truie? Hopefully, your curiosity is piqued for Eddie and Jess…

Make sure to grab their story so you don't miss out!

In all likelihood, the release date will move up... as long as the dark rain clouds cooperate.

Playlist

Find the complete playlist for Out of the Darkness on Spotify.

- Drag Me Out - Archers
- Tonight (demo) - Amira Elfeky
- The Death of Peace of Mind - Bad Omens
- Mine - Sleep Token
- Sign of Life - Motionless In White
- I Like You Best - Ella Reed
- Please Don't Cry - Kami Kehoe
- Under My Skin - Ash to Eden
- Obsessed - Jules
- Shame On Me - Catch Your Breath
- Beg (On Your Knees) - Ash to Eden

Playlist

- IDWT$ - Bad Omens
- Spin In The Dark - The Bela Vibe

Acknowledgments

The two-week diversion turned into a one-off book, that's turned into a wild and dirty ride. When I wrote Into the Woods, I kind of had a feeling that I would give Truie and Teague (Piglet and Tigger) a chance to tell their story. It was tough, I'm not going to lie. I fought with the characters. I fought with myself, questioning everything I wrote. I gave up more times than you can imagine.

How do write a *happily ever after* for someone who has been through hell and hell still lives inside their head? How do you make things right? An over the top, gooey on the inside, and totally gone for her hero... That and an immeasurable amount of patience and a complete lack of compunction when it comes to avenging his hummingbird.

Thanks always to Stacy for this gorgeous cover... Thank you! To Hadley Finn for what might be my best editing experience ever, and Hazel James for putting final eyes on it and sprinkling in little bits of love. And to my girls, my besties, my people. Without you, I would be so damn lost. I love you!

And of course, my family. I couldn't do this without you. All my love!

Also by KC Enders

To laugh, cry, and curse her name, dive into her other titles. *The most current information can be found on her website. For updates and to stay in the know, be sure to sign up for her newsletter.*

Troubles

Twist

Tombstones

Beekman Hills: the series

In Tune

Off Bass

Beat Down

Out Loud (*still* coming soon)

Tattered Hearts

Sweet on You

Into the Woods

About the Author

KC Enders thrives on strong coffee, good bourbon, and the anguished tears of unsuspecting readers. Every now and then, she sprinkles in a good laugh to balance out the shredding of hearts.

To laugh, cry, and curse her name, dive into her other titles. *The most current information can be found on her website.*

She loves talking books, hearing from readers, and hosting the occasional virtual Happy Hour in her Facebook readers' group.

        facebook.com/kcewrites
        instagram.com/authorkcenders
        bookbub.com/profile/kc-enders
        tiktok.com/@kcenderswrites

www.ingramcontent.com/pod-product-compliance
Lightning Source LLC
LaVergne TN
LVHW010309070526
838199LV00065B/5492